Saltwater Falls

Press

Pittsburgh

SALTWATER FALLS

ANJ Press, First edition. March 2021.

Copyright © 2021 Amelia Addler.

Written by Amelia Addler.

Cover design by Charmaine Ross at CharmaineRoss.com

Maps by Nate Taylor at IllustratorNate.com

For the courage to leap

Recap and Introduction to *Saltwater Falls*

Another Clifton family adventure on San Juan Island...

Previously in the Westcott Bay series, Margie Clifton started a new life on the island after her brother Mike, an FBI agent, gifted her his home and barn. Margie turned the barn at Saltwater Cove into a wedding and events business, and made the house a home for her family.

Meanwhile, her daughter Jade worked diligently to create a new state park on San Juan, even suffering retaliation when her house was burned down – though luckily, her beau Matthew was there to save her.

Jade's sister Tiffany and half sister Morgan also helped with developing the park, particularly when an embezzling scheme threatened to tank the state's park budget. Though the parks employee responsible was caught, the senator he was working with, Cathy Shields, walked free.

It seemed that life on the island was about to calm down – until Margie and Chief Hank got into a moped accident. Hank broke his leg, and Margie ended up with a broken hip, ribs and elbow! Connor, who until then was leading a nomad's life and working in beautiful spots across the country, decided it was time to come home and be responsible.

He returns to San Juan Island to help his mom and starts working at a luxury resort to save some money. He's surprised to uncover concerning happenings on the island, and unfortunately, one of the resort's prettiest clients is tangled in the web...

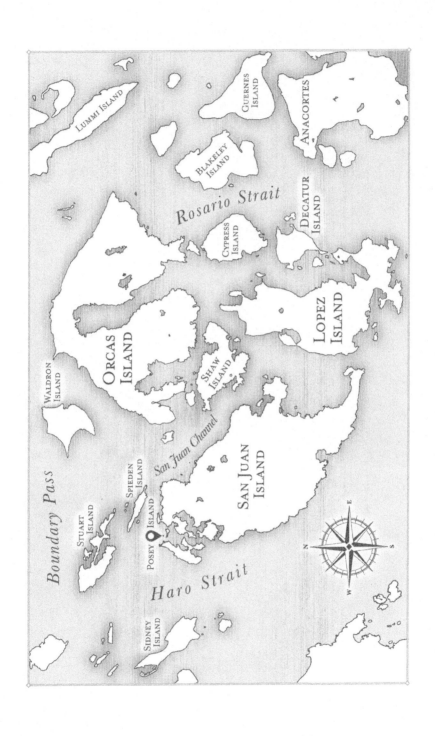

Chapter 1

"So do you not care about the difference between sparkling water and seltzer, or are you just stupid?"

Connor forced himself to smile; it was always easier to do when he could imagine that the person insulting him was an enraged toddler, and not a full-grown adult.

This guy, luckily, resembled an overgrown baby – his round and firm belly protruded over his pants, leaving his shirt's buttons clinging desperately, stretched to their limits. He even had a bib tucked under his collar, with crumbs and flecks of grease speckled all over.

Connor grabbed the bottle of water. "Oh, so sorry about that, I'll be right back with the..."

The man glared at him. "Seltzer! I ordered *seltzer*!"

"Of course." Connor nodded. Now he was beyond a forced smile; he had to stop himself from laughing in the guy's face. "The seltzer."

Truth be told, Connor had no idea what the difference between seltzer and sparkling water even was. Nor did he care to find out, though apparently this was going to be a sticking point for this particular guest.

"Hey Midge – do we have seltzer water?"

She laughed. "Of course we do. Let me guess – Mr. Egan screamed at you for bringing him sparkling water?"

Connor nodded. "Yep."

"He did the same thing to Kayleigh yesterday."

"Ah, so that's why she asked me to take his table."

"Yeah." Midge let out a sigh. "I found her crying in the cooler at the end of the night. So that was nice of you."

Connor accepted the bottle of water from her and squinted at the label. "Hm. I was thinking it'd be fun to bring sparkling water again. Do we have another brand?"

"No."

"Okay, maybe flat water, something with a nice-looking label?"

Midge laughed as she handed him a new glass. "You can try, but it'll be *your* funeral."

Connor rolled his eyes. He was still getting used to the nuances of working at a luxury resort with luxury-minded guests. Unusual requests didn't bother him – in fact, some of them were amusing. Like the guy who said he'd only drink water from a particular spring in Canada. He had a pallet of the stuff shipped in, and the staff had to keep it in a separate fridge, running to get it every time he called.

Other requests weren't as funny – especially when shouting was involved. At first he'd thought that these events were infrequent, but he was seeing them more now that he was closer to full time hours as a server at the resort restaurant.

Initially, he'd worked part-time so that he could help his mom during her recovery from her moped accident. She didn't like being helped or driven around, of course, but he was more than happy to do it and she at least tolerated his help.

Yet even his mom, who was in immense pain with her broken hip, ribs and elbow, never complained like some of these people. She had every right to be grumpy, but rarely got close to losing her temper.

There was that one time when she tried to sneak into the kitchen and ended up dropping her favorite mixing bowl, shattering it to pieces. Connor ran when he heard the commotion and found her in tears, cursing herself and her injuries.

Luckily a little humor went a long way, and after he'd cleaned it up and promised to buy her another one, she apologized for her "outburst."

It was a *very* little outburst. The ones he'd seen here far surpassed it; he'd never seen so many divas in all of his life. But this job was good enough, at least for now – the pay was okay, and occasionally the tips were big.

"My apologies sir, I've got your seltzer here."

The man grunted and waved him away.

Ah.

He'd moved on from yelling to sulking. Fair enough. For Connor, it was all part of the same process – it was like the stages of grief, but instead it was the stages of an adult tantrum.

Connor knew that he was alone in this, but his favorite stage was the yelling. Having another adult yell at him was hilarious. Sometimes, like today, he had to force himself not to burst into laughter; it would only get him into more trouble and prolong the hysterics.

But the fact that a full grown adult could become so angry – *livid*, even – because they received the wrong condiment, the wrong type of water, or because the vegetables weren't prepared to their liking was endlessly amusing, at least to Connor.

Sure, some people said that Connor didn't take life seriously enough – and he could acknowledge that *perhaps* they had a point. But these people were the other end of the spectrum, ridiculous in the opposite direction, taking everything so seriously that they launched their blood pressure sky-high multiple times a day.

Had Mr. Egan ever been to Montana and marveled at the unending, blue sky? Had he ever looked at Mt. Rainier and felt awe? Heck – had he even looked out of the window to see the sunset over the water at this beautiful resort?

Probably not. And it was wishful thinking for Connor to imagine that *anything* could change the man – no, the man-baby. The legend.

Baby Egan.

He snapped out of his daydream to take entrées to his other table. This was a younger couple, in their thirties, who had been staying at the resort for about a week. They ate all of their meals at the resort restaurant, sitting across from each other in silence, scrolling through their phones. It didn't seem like a relaxing vacation to Connor, but what did he know? At least they didn't shout.

"Boy!" bellowed a voice from across the room. "Are you going to keep me waiting here all day?"

Connor looked up to see that Baby Egan needed attention again. He walked over quickly, prepared for the next rant. "Yes sir?"

The man huffed. "My coffee is freezing."

"I'm happy to freshen that up for you, sir."

"And I've been waiting for my check for *hours*."

That seemed unlikely, as he'd only been there about half an hour and inhaled his food in five minutes. "My apologies, I'll grab that as well."

He grunted. "Your apologies are completely worthless. All you've done is apologize."

Connor stood for a moment, unsure how to respond without provoking more wrath, when another voice spoke up from behind him.

"He's been apologizing, but it's *you* who is extremely rude."

Connor turned his head to see a young woman, one table behind them, looking up from her book and addressing Baby Egan directly.

"Excuse me?"

She cleared her throat. "I said: *you* have been extremely rude. If anything, you should be the one apologizing."

Baby Egan ripped the bib out of his shirt and threw it on the table. He took in a gasp of air before puffing it out again, his face growing redder by the second. "I have it – who do you even – I cannot *believe* the treatment that I am – "

"I will not take your abuse," the woman said coolly, still holding her book. "You've behaved abominably. I hope that you do get your check soon so that we can all have a little peace and quiet."

The man stood, fists at his side, and it looked as though he might rush toward her; the moment passed, however, and instead he stood and jabbed his finger into the air. "I have half a mind to get you kicked out of here for talking to me like that."

She shrugged and turned back to her book. "You can try."

He took a step toward her and Connor finally shook off his astonishment, stepping between them. "Please, sir. I'll get your check now, and allow me to prepare a latte to go – on the house, of course."

He crossed his arms, still staring daggers at the back of the woman's head. "Make sure it's with soy milk."

"Of course, soy milk. Coming right up."

Connor almost sprinted to the register to prepare the receipt and saw that Midge was already making the latte.

"It's in *everyone's* best interest if he gets out of here as soon as possible," she said in a low voice.

Connor thanked her before rushing to give Baby Egan the latte and the check.

"You know," Baby Egan said as he stood up again, the redness receding from his face in splotchy patches, "I see a lot of potential in you. Keep working hard and maybe you can get out of this place."

Connor smiled. "Thanks so much, have a good rest of your day, and please let me know if there is *anything* else that we can do for you."

Once Baby Egan was safely out of the restaurant, Connor looked down to see what sort of tip he'd left.

Two dollars.

Oh boy. Not only a kind man, but a generous one, too.

Connor stuffed the money into his pocket before going to check in on his other table and apologize for the commotion.

The woman almost smiled. "No problem at all. That was one of the most entertaining things I've seen here."

"Can I get you anything else?"

She looked back at her phone. "No, we're fine."

He was about to go back to talk to Midge when he noticed a set of eyes peering at him from behind a book. As soon as he saw it, though, the eyes snapped back behind the pages.

Connor looked around – there was almost no one else there. He could spare a minute to talk to her.

He walked over to his savior's table. "I'm sorry that he was so disruptive and impolite to you."

She looked up at him. "Oh – he wasn't disrupting *me* at all. I'm sorry that he was so awful to *you*."

"It's quite all right," Connor heard himself saying. At times, he felt like this job was turning him into a polite robot; he just repeated the same phrases over and over, a smile frozen on his face. Meanwhile, his mind was hundreds of miles away... "I'd like to offer you a complementary – "

She put up a hand. "No, it's really okay. I don't need anything. But thank you."

He nodded and walked back to the server station. It was nice of her to intervene, but he certainly didn't need it. It wasn't yelling that bothered him. What actually upset him were the people who treated him like...well, like he didn't exist and like he didn't matter.

It was the ones who never looked him in the eye, or who ordered him around like a servant. There was this one woman who brought her little dog into the restaurant, sat him atop a chair, and fed him bits of meat and mashed potatoes with a spoon. She called Connor over, and without even looking at him, said, "My dog lost his squeaky bone. Find it."

It was these kind of people that made him feel small; those were the moments that he questioned his worth in the world.

Though apparently, Baby Egan thought he had some worth. No – he thought he had *potential*. Not enough potential to warrant more than a two dollar tip, but potential nonetheless.

Connor wasn't so sure about his "potential" these days. He'd spent the three years after college trying to avoid whatever prospects he had and what he was going to do with his life. He didn't *want* to grow up and get a real job – and he'd managed to travel around the country and avoid it long enough. It was time for him to face the facts: he was too old to keep living like that.

And now, embarrassingly, he didn't even know the difference between sparkling and seltzer water?

Unforgivable.

"Thanks for taking his table today," Kayleigh said, joining him at the server station. "He bit my head off yesterday. But thankfully, I hear he's checking out of the resort."

"That's good news," Connor said.

"Is she a friend of yours or something?" Kayleigh nodded toward the woman who was still reading her book.

Connor shook his head. "No, I've never met her before."

"Oh, good." She leaned in and lowered her voice. "Because she asked me where we all like to hang out, saying she'd like to make some friends on the island."

Connor instinctively pulled away from Kayleigh – he didn't like gossiping, especially in earshot of the guests. And her perfume was...unpleasant. "Oh?"

Kayleigh scoffed. "Yeah, like what does she think this is? *Dirty Dancing*? And she's going to go and hang out with the staff and then run back to her rich daddy?"

"Well, that's not really – "

Kayleigh cut him off. "I told her that she could meet us at the falls tomorrow. The saltwater falls."

Connor shot a look over at the woman – she wasn't *that* far away, and she could probably hear them. "I don't think that – "

"Oh relax." She let out a snorting laugh. "She'll never find it!"

Kayleigh walked off and left Connor standing there. He didn't mind taking a difficult guest to help her out, but he also didn't want to be a part of her bullying.

Connor wasn't as bitter toward the wealthy guests as some of his coworkers were – or at least he tried not to be.

But now what was going to happen? This woman would go around asking people where the saltwater falls were, and get made fun of behind her back?

He let out a sigh. On the one hand, he didn't want to anger Kayleigh and the rest of his coworkers by inviting a guest to hang out with them. Technically, they could get fired for that – so in that way, it kind of *was* like *Dirty Dancing*.

His sisters had only made him watch that movie once, though, and he didn't remember how it turned out. But he didn't like how Kayleigh was acting, and he didn't want her thinking that he was on her side.

Besides, this poor woman was just trying to be friendly. What was so bad about that? Connor knew what it was like, coming to a new place; sometimes he'd arrive at a site for a new seasonal job and not know a soul. He always ended up with a group of friends by the end of the season, though.

Granted, the attitude of the staff at the resort so far hadn't been all that friendly. It might not win him any points to help a guest out...

But she'd helped him first, and he wanted to return the favor. He straightened his shoulders and made his way to her table.

Chapter 2

It finally felt like the adrenaline was clearing from her veins. Teresa wasn't used to standing up to people, but it was something that she had to learn if she wanted to make it anywhere in her new job – and in the film industry in general.

Plus, that guy was being *such* a jerk to that exceptionally cute and overly nice waiter! She'd wanted to say something when she overheard the man's first belittling rant, but it took her a while to build up the courage.

Teresa took a sip of her soda, realizing that her hand was still a bit shaky, and tried to focus her eyes back on her book. She'd been staring at it for some time – hopefully no one noticed that she hadn't turned the page in a while. Her mind was still racing from the confrontation.

All in all, she was pretty proud of how she'd handled it. Her voice didn't quiver, she managed to keep an even tone, and eventually, when she started ignoring the guy, he just left!

There was that tense moment when he was walking out of the restaurant that she thought he might say something to her, but luckily, he seemed quite pleased with his latte and sauntered off.

"Excuse me, miss?"

Teresa nearly jumped out of her chair. For a moment, she was afraid that the man had come back and was going to start screaming at her. She was relieved when she realized that it was just the waiter – who was even cuter close up.

"Oh, hi!"

He smiled. "Hi. So this is kind of awkward..."

Teresa looked around. Uh oh. Was she going to be kicked out of the resort because she'd just yelled at the owner or something? Her parents would be so mad at her... "Oh, I'm sorry, did I cause some sort of trouble?"

He shook his head and dropped his voice. "No, no – not at all. It's just that I overheard you asking Kayleigh about the saltwater falls?"

"Oh, yes."

"I, uh..." He looked down, then back up at her again. "It's just that – well, there are no saltwater falls. I'm really sorry, she thinks it's funny to say that to people. It's just a joke, of course."

She stared at him for a moment. He had the most dazzling white smile – or maybe his teeth looked extra white because he was so tanned? "Oh, I knew that."

"You did?"

She nodded. "I mean – I figured she was pulling my leg. Not that I'm a waterfall expert or anything. I guess I only knew that there were no waterfalls on San Juan Island because I needed to find a waterfall for this movie that we're shooting, and quickly realized it was impossible."

He laughed. "No, there aren't any here. But there are some on Orcas Island."

She nodded. "Right. I wasn't trying to be nosy or anything by asking her about hangouts, she just seemed really nice and I only got here a few days ago...I'm just looking to, you know, make some friends."

He nodded. "Of course. We have a variety of activities for our guests, I can get a pamphlet – "

Teresa shook her head. "No, that's okay. I saw the yoga and...the water aerobics?"

Connor laughed. "Not aerobics, I believe they call it water Zumba."

"Ah, Zumba. Yes." She paused. "I'll pass on that, thank you. I was hoping to explore the island a little. And yeah, I got the feeling that she was making fun of me."

He looked down. His cheeks looked a little flushed. "I'm sorry about that. Really."

"It's okay!" She smiled. "No harm done!"

He looked around before speaking again. "Did you say that you're working on a movie?"

"Yeah! Well – I'm just a location scout. So I'm pretty low on the totem pole. Actually, I don't know if I'm even *on* the totem pole."

He laughed. "That's still really cool."

"Yeah, it's fun."

"I'd love to hear more about it. Are you meeting someone here? Or...are you staying at the resort?"

Teresa tried not to flinch before answering him. Of course he would think it was very odd for a lowly location scout to be staying at the esteemed Whispering Waves Resort. How awkward would it be to explain that her parents insisted that she stay here, and that they insisted on paying? "I'm staying at the resort, actually. My room number is – wait, I keep forgetting the number. But it's under my name, Teresa Timmons."

"Oh."

He looked disappointed and she rushed to add, "But I mean – I really just got here and – "

"No, it's just that we can get in trouble for hanging out with guests – though I'd love to know more about this movie."

"And I would love to see the saltwater waterfalls," she said with a laugh.

He smiled. "It's actually a nickname for this place where we meet up once a month. It's an unusual kind of...tourist attraction. So we don't like everyone to know that we're going there."

She cocked her head to the side. "Oh? I'm always looking for unusual places."

He laughed and scratched the back of his neck. "It's technically...well, it's a mausoleum."

She set her book down. "Wait – really? You hang out with a bunch of dead people?"

"Yeah, we're kind of idiots," he said with a laugh. "The place is cool – kind of creepy, obviously. We hang out and try to scare each other with ghost stories. Actually, the more I talk about this, the dumber it sounds."

A smile spread across Teresa's face. "I don't think so. I think that it sounds awesome."

"Well, how about this. Let me get you another soda or something? I can discreetly give you my phone number and show you around. As long as you promise not to tell anyone."

"My lips are sealed!"

He smiled at her before walking away.

Well!

Teresa didn't want to get this guy in trouble, but talk about fortune favoring the bold! She worked up the courage to stand up to that bully, and now she might've made her first friend on San Juan Island! What could be better?

As promised, he got her another soda and with a wink slipped her a small piece of paper with his phone number. She was about to save the number into her phone when she realized that she didn't know his name. Teresa was just about to ask him when her phone started ringing.

Her stomach dropped. It was Chet, her boss. No – not even her boss, her boss's boss's boss!

"Hello?"

"It's me. I need to know what you've got for my opener."

She cleared her throat. "Oh, did you see the email that I sent you this morning? I had four new locations, and I – "

"No I didn't. I guess I'll go look."

The call dropped. Teresa pulled the phone away from her face to make sure that she hadn't accidentally ended the call.

Nope. He'd just hung up on her. Why was he always doing that? Couldn't he at least say goodbye?

No matter. If he didn't like any of the locations that she'd found for him, maybe this mausoleum would work? Or maybe her new friend could tell her about some other spots on the island.

She sat back and clasped her hands together; the warmth had returned to her fingers at last. Things were certainly looking up! She couldn't wait to see this mausoleum, and whatever else this island had in store.

Chapter 3

On Sunday morning, Connor worked an early shift to help with the breakfast and brunch rush; once that was through, he had the rest of the day to himself.

There was a baby shower scheduled at the barn at Saltwater Cove later that afternoon, so as soon as his shift was done, he went to see his mom and help her set up.

Morgan and Jade were already there putting up some tables, much to his mom's dismay.

"I don't want you girls lifting all of these heavy tables!" she said, standing helplessly in the doorway, leaning on her cane.

"Oh Margie, we're fine!" Morgan said. "Don't you usually do this by yourself anyway?"

"No, Hank helps me. And I hate seeing you girls do it. And I hate that everyone – "

"Yeah, we know Mom. You hate ever having to accept help from anyone," Connor said, planting a kiss on her cheek.

She let out a huff. "Mothers should help their children, not the other way around."

"While that might be true," said Jade, "it's on hold when a mother falls off of a moped."

Connor suppressed a smile as he helped Morgan carry the largest table across the floor.

"My mom always used to yell at me when I picked up heavy things," said Morgan. "She'd be like, 'Stop! You're going to break your baby maker!'"

They managed to set the table down just as Connor started losing his grip from laughter.

"She was right!" his mom yelled from across the room. "Now stop. Everything is just fine where it is. I can arrange the rest."

Connor shook his head. They were getting close to wedding season and he was seeing how difficult it would be to keep his mom from re-injuring herself. "No way Mom. We're not letting you move anything, and that's final."

She stood for a moment, looking like she was going to argue with him, but thankfully, she gave in.

It had been a tough year for her – between turning fifty and breaking all of those bones, things hadn't been easy. She was always talking about how she never expected to get old "all of a sudden."

Connor disagreed about her being old; she wasn't old at all! She'd just had an unfortunate accident, and recovery was taking as long as expected – that is, a few months.

But he understood her frustration, especially as someone who was used to doing everything not only for herself but for everyone around her. She wasn't used to accepting help in any way, and that was a hard habit to break.

Connor was thankful that Chief's daughter Amanda had also moved back to San Juan to help after their parents' accident. While Connor was more than happy to help his mom in every way possible, sometimes it was better to have Amanda there to help his mom with things like getting in and out of the shower and getting dressed.

If Connor had helped in those instances, they both might've died of embarrassment. Amanda, however, handled it with grace. She'd also managed to get her job transferred to

Seattle from London so she could stay for a few months. Her job seemed demanding – much more so than Connor's – but she handled that with ease, too.

It did not escape Connor that all of his sisters were so much better at handling responsibility than he was. He was going to change that, though. And soon.

And fortunately, it seemed that his mom was well on the way to recovery. Connor was grateful that she was *able* to recover – and that her accident didn't leave her permanently disabled, or worse – dead!

For weeks after the accident, Connor couldn't put his finger on why he felt so uneasy about it all. After all, she was going to be fine.

But after a while, he realized it was because he had to face the fact that his mom really *could have died*. That was terrifying and something that he'd never seriously considered before. It just seemed impossible! How could his mom die? She was all-knowing and invincible! She couldn't die in a moped accident like a regular human.

But the accident reminded him that that was wishful thinking. And as much as he insisted that she was not old, it also made him realize that one day, she actually *would* get old. And then what?

He wanted to be in a position in his life where he could help take care of her (no matter how much she would complain about it). There was no way that he'd be able to do that if he was still working minimum wage jobs, hopping from national parks to horse ranches and ski resorts.

"What's wrong honey?"

Connor snapped out of his thoughts and looked up. "Oh, nothing Mom."

"Don't lie to me, I can tell something is wrong. You have an intense frown on your face."

He smiled. "It's nothing, I promise. I was just thinking about some stuff."

"What kind of stuff?"

He shrugged. "I don't know."

She looked at him for a moment before speaking again. "I've told you that you don't have to stick around here and put your life on hold to take care of me. I feel bad enough as it is, and – "

"No Mom, it's nothing like that. I swear. My life isn't on hold at all. It's really just that..."

"What? What's the matter? Did something happen at work?"

He shook his head. "No. I just...my life is on hold because I don't know what to do next. That's all."

"Oh. I see. So you missed your window for summer jobs because of me."

He laughed. "No! I can't do that stuff anymore. I need to find a real job. That's the problem."

"Ah," she said, nodding. "Well I can't do much in the barn, but I can get on the computer and look for jobs for you!"

Connor groaned. "No, please don't do that. I'm an adult, I can't have my mom applying to jobs for me."

"You can do the applying, I'll just send them your way."

He shook his head. "Thank you for the offer, but I don't even know what I'm looking for yet. That's all. Don't worry so much, okay?"

"Fine," she said with a sigh.

She still looked sad, so he went and gave her a hug. His mom was a big hugger. "I love being here with you and getting to spend time with everyone. Really. Even if it wasn't under the best circumstances."

She smiled. "You can say that again. My physical therapist says that I'm doing great, though. He's really impressed with how well I'm walking. He said I might not need the cane soon!"

"Good!"

Morgan and Jade finished up a few last touches and they all headed back to the house to have some tea. His mom insisted on making the tea herself and sent them away to sit in the living room.

"How's construction going on the new park?" asked Connor. "Running into any other issues?"

Jade shook her head. "Not really. I mean, things pop up here and there, but nothing major. There was an issue getting some of the limestone unloaded, but we sorted that out last week."

Morgan cut in. "I mean, I'm glad that nothing else bad has happened, but I'm always paranoid that something more is just around the corner."

"What do you mean?" asked Connor.

"I don't know," she said with a shrug. "I guess I'm waiting for the other shoe to drop. I mean, first they tried to kill Jade and burned down our house, and then we found out that a parks employee was in on some shady deal with a senator, and he almost bankrupted the whole state parks department. And now there's just...nothing?"

"I'm not trying to tempt fate here!" said Jade. "If everything else goes smoothly, then I'll be grateful."

"But what if it's just the calm before the storm? It's not like Senator Shields ever got in trouble. So what is she up to now?"

Morgan narrowed her eyes. "Connor – have you seen anything suspicious at work?"

He laughed. "Suspicious? Not really. Unless you count a man insisting that he can only sleep on his own mattress as suspicious."

Her eyes widened. "Are you serious? Did that really happen?"

"Yeah. He overnighted his mattress to the resort so that we would have it ready for him when he arrived. I had to help them carry it up to his room."

Jade shook her head. "That's ridiculous."

Connor shrugged. "It was pretty funny. He was actually really nice – I served him for dinner one night and he tipped me three hundred dollars."

"People are just so much nicer when they get a good night's sleep," Morgan mused.

"That's probably true," said Jade.

"But seriously Connor – I bet there's all kinds of interesting stuff happening at that resort. All kinds of deals being made."

"You have an overactive imagination," Jade said.

"I do not!" Morgan crossed her arms. "Just keep your eyes open. And your ears peeled."

Connor paused. "Do you mean keep my ears open and my eyes peeled?"

"Yeah, that's what I said."

"No you didn't."

She frowned. "Of course it is, what else would I have said?"

"You said keep your ears peeled – "

"Oh my gosh, would you two stop!" Jade said with a laugh.

"I think it's important that we clarify that I can, in fact, speak correctly," said Morgan.

Jade shook her head. "No, I mean stop looking for conspiracies! We finally have some peace and now the two of you are going to go looking for trouble."

Connor leaned back. "I don't go looking for trouble. Trouble comes looking for me."

Morgan snorted. "Did you get that from a movie or something?"

"No, I just thought it sounded cool."

"It did sound pretty cool," she said with a nod.

Jade rolled her eyes. "I'm going to go help Mom carry the tea."

Morgan sat back and put her feet up on the coffee table. "I'm telling you – I don't care *what* Jade says. I know this is just the calm before the storm."

"What storm?"

She sighed. "Just like – you know, the next bad thing."

"I haven't really run into *anything* bad since I've been on the island."

"Famous last words," Morgan said. "And if Senator Shields doesn't make herself known again...then I might just have to go looking for her."

"Don't let Jade hear you say that," Connor said, shooting a look toward the kitchen.

Morgan scrunched her nose. "Jade knows I'm right. It was bizarre that the senator didn't get caught up in the parks scandal. How could she be allowed to play innocent?"

"Probably because she's a senator."

"Yeah..." Morgan nodded, staring off into the distance for a moment before she snapped out of it. "So what're you up to today?"

"Not much. I think I'll hang around here for the rest of the day in case Mom needs any more help, or in case that baby shower gets out of control."

"That would be a first – an out of control baby shower."

"You never know. How about you?"

"I'm just going to be editing some pictures that I took for an engagement shoot. I can do that here if you wanted to go out and do something. I don't mind hanging out with Margie."

"That's nice of you. But no, I don't really have anything to do. Later tonight we're doing ghost stories at the mausoleum again."

Morgan shuddered. "That's so creepy. I can't believe you guys go to that place and just hang out."

"I don't know how it became a tradition, but it's kind of fun. You can come if you want."

"No thank you. I mean, I went there once during the day and I appreciate that the place has a bunch of symbolism and people really like that. But it still creeps me out."

"Suit yourself. Oh actually, that reminds me." Connor pulled out his phone. "I invited one of the resort guests to come and she just texted me asking for directions."

"Ew, she actually wants to go?"

"I guess so."

Morgan made a face. "She probably thought you were kidding. You'd better take her there when it's still light out so she can see how weird it is and have time to leave."

"Do you really think it's that bad?"

"*I* wouldn't want to be there after dark."

Connor paused. She'd seemed excited about it, but maybe Morgan was right. "Okay. Maybe I'll meet her there early and show her around."

"Yeah – give her a chance to change her mind. It's so easy to get lost trying to find that place, too."

"That's true. Maybe I'll tell her that I can meet her at like... seven? If you don't mind hanging around here to help clean up."

"I don't mind at all. And I think Hank will be done with his shift around eight anyway."

"Thanks little sis."

Morgan frowned. "Ugh, you can't call me that. I feel older than you."

He nodded. "You do *seem* older."

"That's right," Morgan said, standing up. "You're the baby of the family, even if you are *a little* older than me. And you'll always be the baby, no matter what you do!"

He couldn't think of a comeback quickly enough before she walked off.

She wasn't wrong. Connor had always been the baby, and it was perhaps worse because he was the only boy in the family. His mom and sisters seemed to really enjoy helping him with things, and Connor, unlike his mom, loved receiving help.

He had no pride in that regard. It defined him in some ways, many of them positive – he was an easygoing team member, he worked well on collective goals and he never got too stuck on his own plans.

Yet in other ways, being the baby was starting to haunt him. He was twenty-five years old and had been pretty much coasting through life until now.

Suddenly it wasn't so cute.

Connor let out a sigh. At least he'd been able to come back and help his mom, and to spend more time with his sisters. Not only did he get the honor of Morgan sharpening her tongue on him; he also got to spend hours upon hours with Amanda as they both, usually unsuccessfully, tried to help their stubborn parents.

Amanda was much tougher than he was, and that was a good thing. Sometimes she yelled at Chief to get him to do what he was supposed to – whether it was going to physical therapy, turning down a shift at work or simply going to the dentist (which Chief decided, at one point, he should get a pass on for a year since he'd seen "so many doctors" recently).

Connor could hear his mom's voice from the kitchen. "I am perfectly able to carry a tea pot, Jade!"

He chuckled to himself and decided to seize this moment of peace to write back to Teresa. He suggested to her that they meet up early so he could show her the mausoleum in the daylight, and she could decide for herself if she wanted to stick around for the ghost stories.

She answered quickly, saying that sounded like a good plan to her, and she appreciated the daylight for taking a few pictures for her boss.

He wasn't really sure what the rules around shooting a movie there would be, but he assumed she must know how all of that worked.

A moment later, Jade and Morgan returned with cups of tea and his mom sat down to join them. They spent some time together before Morgan and Jade had to leave. Once they cleaned up, Connor tried to get his mom to watch a movie with him.

He was, predictably, unsuccessful and instead he busied himself with tidying up the downstairs of the house. He came across an old pamphlet for the mausoleum and decided to give it to Teresa; that way she'd know he wasn't making up all of the history about the place.

It was one small thing he could do in an effort to not creep her out, as Morgan so kindly pointed out he was likely doing.

Hopefully that was enough. He didn't know much about her, other than the fact she seemed to like reading books, making movies and that she had the most eye catching auburn hair...

Chapter 4

After parking her car, Teresa walked over to the trail entrance where Connor said he would meet her. It was quite peaceful, though she felt odd just standing there, listening to the bugs calling out from the trees.

She peered at the time – 7:06. Maybe the cute waiter was pulling a prank on her, too, and he wasn't actually going to show up. Maybe he and the waitress were watching from afar, laughing at her.

It didn't seem likely, but it didn't seem impossible either. Why had her waitress hated her so much? They'd never met before, and Teresa always tried to be nice. Maybe she was just one of those people who hated everybody...

Much to her relief, Teresa spotted someone jogging toward her a moment later.

"I'm so sorry I'm late," he said. "I always park down the street and...well, I'm just not very used to having to be places on time. I'm sorry."

She smiled. "It's no problem at all. Though I have one question before we go and look at this place."

"Sure, anything."

"Well – I never got your name."

He laughed. "Oh, sorry about that. I'm Connor, Connor Clifton."

She stuck out her hand. "It's nice to meet you Connor."

"And you, Teresa Timmons from 302."

She laughed. "Thanks, 302. I *will* remember that."

He cleared his throat. "So it's a little bit of a hike to get to the mausoleum, and I have to warn you – we're also going to pass a cemetery on the way there."

"Sounds good to me. Just...are we *allowed* to be here?"

"Oh yeah!" Connor started walking into the woods and Teresa followed him. "It's completely open to the public. And it's not like any mausoleum you've seen before. It's an enormous monument to this guy's family. Here – I brought you this pamphlet so you'd know that I wasn't making all of this up."

She accepted it from him and studied the picture on the front. "Wow. Wait. That's how it looks?"

It looked more like an ancient Roman ruin than a mausoleum. There were five enormous, white columns – or was it six columns?

"Is one of the columns broken?"

"Yes, good eye," he said, spinning around to dazzle her with another smile. "That broken column was intentionally made that way. The guy who built the place, John McMillan, was a famous businessman here on San Juan Island in the early 1900s. He sold limestone – you'll see the limestone table when we get there."

Teresa smiled. "Sounds exciting."

Connor hopped over a fallen log and then reached out a hand to help her. "Careful – this looks slippery."

"Thanks." Teresa reached out and used his hand to steady herself – totally unnecessary, since she'd worn her hiking boots, but she still liked that he offered and she couldn't just leave him hanging!

"Limestone was as exciting as it got on San Juan Island back in the day. Anyway, John wanted to build this monument for his family, and that broken pillar you see in the picture?

That's meant to symbolize how we often die before our work on earth is complete."

Teresa stopped. "You're kidding."

He put his hands up. "I swear! Go ahead, I think it's in the pamphlet."

She gave him a side eye and opened the pamphlet. On the second page, there was a paragraph explaining it – Connor was telling the truth. "Hm. Okay, so this is actually living up to being as weird as I thought it would be."

He laughed. "So in the center of all of the columns is a huge limestone table, and around the table are six chairs, made of solid stone and cement. Those are the crypts for the ashes of the McMillan family."

Teresa's jaw dropped. "Oh my gosh! I'm getting goose bumps! This is so...serious."

"Yeah, McMillan didn't mess around. He has them all sitting there together for eternity. And the sun shines through that broken pillar and unites them for all time."

"That guy was *intense*."

"Tell me about it."

She slowed down, seeing the cemetery that Connor had promised. "And what about these tombstones here? Do they mean something too?"

Connor peered over at the pamphlet in her hands. "That I'm not too sure of, actually."

"Okay, it's actually better that there's just a regular cemetery and it's not some crazy voodoo stuff."

Before too long, they reached the site of the mausoleum. It was just as quiet and peaceful as the rest of the forest, but Teresa felt that it was somehow more still. Maybe she was imagining it? There was no one else there, and after walking through the woods for so long, it felt strange to stumble upon such an enormous structure. She stood, looking straight up and feeling like a tourist.

Connor pointed ahead of them. "You see these stairs? The first flight has three steps; they represent the three ages of man. The second flight right here has five steps which represents... something else."

Teresa laughed. "It says here in my pamphlet that the five steps are for the five orders of classic architecture and the five senses. And the last flight of seven steps are for the seven liberal arts and sciences, and the days of the week."

"That's right!" He clapped his hands together. "I swear I'm usually a much better tour guide."

She thought he was doing *just* fine. "Do you often give tours?"

Connor pulled his hands out from his jean pockets and crossed them over his chest. Teresa tried not to stare at his muscles.

"I used to. There was a summer where I did hiking tours and overnight camping trips in the Rocky Mountains."

"That's so cool!"

"It was really cool. I also spent a summer at Lake Tahoe. I did kayaking tours there. I'm still pretty new to San Juan Island, though, so I'm still learning about the history."

"Well, I'm thoroughly impressed," said Teresa. "Did you just come here on a whim, then?"

Connor shook his head. "No. I have family here. My mom and my sisters." He let out a sigh. "My mom was in a moped accident a few months ago, so I came back to help her recover."

"Oh my gosh, that's terrible! Is she okay?"

"Yeah, she had some broken bones, but she's getting better every day. I think what annoys her the most is that her kids have to help her."

"Yes, that would be too much for any mother," Teresa said. "So after this are you going to live in the Grand Canyon or something?"

He laughed. "No. I think it's time for me to finally grow up and get a real job. One where I can't show up in shorts and sandals. I might even have to buy a tie, I'm not really sure."

"Ah. That doesn't sound like fun."

He scratched the back of his neck. "Yeah, it doesn't, which is why I've been avoiding it. I went to school for biology, so I could probably get a job working in a lab somewhere."

"But you don't want to do that?"

He shrugged. "The problem was that I found out too late that I *really* hate working in labs. I love being outside."

"Can't you study, like, rivers or watersheds or something?"

"Probably not, unless I go back and get a doctorate. Which I'm not terribly interested in doing, either."

Teresa nodded. "That's tough."

"Did you go to school for filmmaking?" he asked.

"Sort of. Well – yes. I double majored in film and pre-law. My parents are both attorneys, as are both of my older brothers. So my parents are dead set on me becoming an attorney, too, and joining the family law firm."

"Oh, those are...pretty different majors."

"I know. But film is what I've always wanted to do. I really want to get into editing – you know, postproduction stuff. But it's not been easy."

"I can only imagine."

Teresa leaned against one of the pillars. How much did she really need to tell Connor about her current situation? She'd probably bore him to death.

But it felt like there was no one in her life that really understood what she was doing. And he might think that she was crazy, too. All of her friends from school were doing the responsible thing – they were going on to get jobs, or applying to law school.

At least Connor admitted that he didn't want to grow up. Maybe that was her problem, too?

He stepped closer to her. "But it seems like you're doing pretty well if you're working on a movie, right?"

Teresa let out a sigh. "Well, it's my first one, outside of school or little projects that I've done. I just graduated and my parents were really disappointed when I didn't apply to law school right away. They made a deal with me – that I could have one year to try to make it in the film industry, and they would support me. But after that, if it didn't happen, I'd have to go to law school."

"That's a lot of pressure for one year," he said with a smile. "I've been living the nomad life for *three* years, and I still don't know what to do with myself."

She laughed. "I know. And it's really embarrassing because they're so afraid of letting me out of their sight. I grew up in a really small town, and there was no crime at all. Like the reason that I'm staying at the resort is because..." She closed her eyes. "Because they think it's safe and they don't want me to be living in a van or starving, so they're paying for it."

"Okay, so your parents are loaded then."

Teresa laughed. "Yeah. They've been very successful with their law firm. And they just don't understand why I don't want to follow in their footsteps."

"What type of law do they practice?"

"Taxes. It's all tax stuff. So, super boring."

"Yeah..." Connor said slowly. "That doesn't sound great."

Teresa walked to the center of the mausoleum, running a hand on the back of one of the cement chairs.

"There's a name on here – is this one of his kids?"

Connor nodded. "Yeah. He had his whole family placed here with him. Except for one son, I think."

Teresa frowned. "Well that's pretty weird."

"I mean, I don't know what the son did. Maybe he was a jerk, or he started a different limestone company, or – "

She shook her head. "No, I mean that his kids are all entombed here with him. I mean – didn't they have families of their own? Where did their spouses and kids go? What if they wanted to be with their own families?"

Connor laughed. "I don't know, and I never really thought about it that way."

"Hm." She stood for a moment, staring at the chair in front of her. "I guess it's not a new thing, then, for parents to struggle with their kids having lives of their own."

He smiled. "I guess not."

Maybe the other son refused to sell limestone and instead followed his dreams. The thought made her smile. "What about you? Do your parents put a lot of pressure on you to grow up and get a 'real' job?"

Connor shook his head. "No, not at all. My parents never really tried to influence us in any way. I mean, my mom was really supportive during school; she helped a lot and encouraged us to do what we liked."

"Oh. That sounds great."

He nodded. "Yeah, she is great. But I've been doing all of these really fun jobs for the last few years, and now I don't have anything. I don't have any money saved, I don't have a career. I barely have a working car."

Teresa looked away and tried to appear distracted by the names on the backs of the chairs. She knew what he was saying; he didn't have rich parents to pay for him to follow his dreams.

Teresa was acutely aware that she was spoiled and extremely lucky. Her parents had paid for her to go to school – well, they'd paid for all of her living expenses, because she'd won several scholarships and managed to piece together tuition and fees with those. But now they were paying for her to live at a five star resort – it was ridiculous!

She was mortified by it, but her mom was certain that nowhere else was safe. Compared to where Teresa had grown up in Norwich, Ontario, sure, everything seemed unsafe. That was small-town living.

It didn't help that the first time her mom had been to the US was for a visit to Detroit when she was a teenager. She and some of her friends decided to make a little road trip, and decades later, she talked about how she saw a guy with a hand-gun, and how it was the scariest moment of her life. It seems that over the years, her story morphed from simply catching a glimpse of the handgun to it actually being brandished at one of her friends.

Her mom was therefore *convinced* that the same situation would happen to her beloved daughter, even on safe little San Juan Island. Her fears were borderline neurotic, despite Teresa assuring her that she'd never even *seen* a handgun in real life. It didn't matter; the news stressed that nowhere was safe and that was that.

Teresa was embarrassed by how over-protective her mom was, and by how much money her parents wasted on her, and by how silly her dreams of working on movies sounded – she was ashamed of all of it. She loved her parents and didn't want to worry or disappoint them, but sometimes she wished that she could just disappear and live in the mountains like Connor.

Though that didn't seem like it was going very well for him either.

"It's not true that you don't have anything," she said. "You clearly have a lot of skills. And you know what you like, which is a lot more than most people can say."

He shrugged. "I guess. So what's this movie that you're working on?"

"It's not really a genre that I'm *crazy* about," she said slowly. "But we've got a great team, and I think we're doing some exciting things. The title is *Zombies in the Sand*."

He nodded. "Okay, a zombie movie. I like it. Who's the director? Anyone that I know?"

"Probably not, he's pretty new. His name is Chet Laret."

Connor stopped. "Wait a second – is he staying at the resort too?"

Teresa nodded. "Yeah, you might've seen him. He's one of those creative, big personality type guys."

"Yeah – I think I know him. I didn't know his name, though. I think I've seen it written down, but I thought his last name was pronounced La-rett. I thought it was funny that it rhymed."

Teresa laughed. "That's a *grave* mistake – he wants people to say it the French way: La-ray. I don't think that he's French, but – whatever. He's the director, what he says, goes."

"Very cool, I can accept that!" Connor said, putting his hands up.

"And he also wrote the script...and is the lead actor."

Connor looked at her, smiling broadly. "Oh, I see. So I'm guessing this isn't really a big-budget kind of movie?"

She shook her head. "No, and I know that all sounds really lame, but this is a real, legitimate movie! It's about a zombie attack on an island, and I've been really impressed with the team that we have for this project. I mean, I met some of the special effects people, like the people who are going to make the actors look like zombies. And they're incredible! Real professionals with a lot of experience, so, I'm hoping this works out. Especially considering my time constraints..."

Connor put a hand up. "I'm sorry, I didn't mean to insult it or anything, I don't know anything about movies."

"It's okay," she said with a smile. "It's not like anything you could say would be more critical than what my parents have already said about it."

"That's tough. Well – for your sake, I hope it's a success."

She smiled. "Thanks. I was actually thinking I'd take some pictures of this place for a potential scene. Chet likes to be involved in all of those decisions. Sometimes he wants me to give him like ten options, and then he ends up taking the first one anyway."

"Ah yes, a creative soul."

She laughed. "Yeah. So I brought my camera actually and I was thinking – "

Her phone went off. "Oh my gosh, I'm so sorry. It's my boss calling, do you mind if I – ?"

"Not at all! Please."

She smiled at him before answering. "Hello?"

"Teresa, I just talked to Chet."

It was Liv, the producer.

"What's up?"

"He said you're one bad location away from getting canned."

Oh boy. She felt like she was going to throw up. She took a seat on one of the mausoleum chairs. "I thought that he'd like the new places that I sent, the ones from yesterday – "

"I know, I'm just telling you. He said that none of those locations were good enough for the zombie wedding. If you don't get him someplace by noon tomorrow, you're gone."

"Okay, I'll get right on that."

"Good luck."

She put the phone back in her purse and realized that Connor was staring at her. "Is everything okay?"

"Uh – sort of. My first job might be cut short."

"What's wrong?"

She rubbed her face in her hands. "It's me, it's my fault. I was supposed to get a location where we could shoot this wedding scene where the zombies disrupt the vows. You know, like right when they ask if anyone objects?"

Connor nodded.

"It's supposed to be like a zombie running in then," she said, shaking her head. "And anyway, every place I went on the island, I was too shy when I talked to the people and they all said no, so I only had two locations that I found and they're just restaurants and..."

"You went to *all* of the wedding venues on the island?"

"I went to a lot, but sometimes I have a hard time being assertive – or more like, forward and convincing, you know? Like really selling the idea of the movie being shot at someone's house or business and...oh, I don't know. I messed it all up."

A smile spread across Connor's face. "I might have the answer to your problems."

Chapter 5

It took some time to convince her, but Margie was able to get Morgan to go home.

"Hank will be here in half an hour. Do you really think I can't be left unattended for half an hour?"

Morgan narrowed her eyes. "I don't trust you not to go into the barn and try to clean everything up by yourself, that's all."

Margie sighed. "I can do a *bit* of light cleaning! I promise I won't move any of the furniture."

After a moment, Morgan said, "Fine."

Margie was busy pulling the tablecloths off of the tables when her phone rang. Connor!

"Hi honey!"

"Hey Mom. I'm on my way to see you – I have a favor to ask."

"Oh, did the ghost stories scare you too much? Should I make some hot chocolate and get your favorite Dr. Seuss book like when you were little?"

He laughed. "No, it's nothing like that."

Margie chuckled to herself. Connor had a lot of trouble with restless nights when he was ten or so. The hot chocolate was always her last resort. "So what's up?"

"Well..." There was a moment of silence. "How do you feel about the barn being used in a movie?"

That certainly wasn't something she was expecting him to ask. "Ah – in a movie? What kind of movie?"

"It's a zombie movie that's being shot here on the island."

"Are you making this movie with your friends?"

"No, I'm not involved – not really. I made a new friend who's working on the crew – it's her job to find places to shoot different scenes. They have a scene where zombies attack a wedding or something and they can't find anywhere good to film it."

"I see."

"She's going to end up in trouble...and I thought that maybe she could take some pictures of the barn as a possible location, if that's okay with you?"

Margie looked around. There were still a few baby shower decorations hanging up. "Well it's kind of a mess in here."

"That's okay! I can clean it up."

"And I don't have any makeup on!"

Connor laughed. "Don't worry Mom – you wouldn't have to be in the pictures. But would you mind? If the barn ended up being in the movie?"

"I don't think so. As long as they don't need it on a day we have an event planned. And they don't leave a mess."

"I don't think they would leave a mess," said Connor.

"Then..." Margie looked around. She didn't love the idea, but if it was to help one of Connor's friends, she had no objections. "Let's give it a shot, I guess!"

"You're the best, Mom! My phone is about to die, but we'll be there in a few minutes."

He wasn't kidding about only being a few minutes away; Margie had enough time to clean off two more tables before

Connor appeared in the doorway of the barn, closely followed by a pretty young woman.

Margie smiled and waved them over. Connor walked right in, while the young woman hung back a bit, hands clasped in front of her, taking small steps.

In that moment, she reminded Margie of a dainty ballerina. As she got closer, Margie could make out her beautiful green eyes and delicate features.

No wonder Connor wanted to help out this *particular* friend. She was as cute as a button!

Margie tried not to stare at her. "Hi, welcome!"

"Hey Mom," said Connor. "This is my friend Teresa, the one that I was telling you about?"

The girl rushed forward to offer a handshake. "It's so nice to meet you Mrs. Clifton!"

"It's nice to meet you too, Teresa. Welcome to my humble barn!"

Teresa looked up, her eyes tracing the rafters and lingering on the bistro lights. "It's absolutely stunning!"

"Thank you very much," said Margie, studying her. "I hear that you're making a zombie movie?"

Teresa nodded. "Yes – I'm on the crew, at least. So basically – how this works – I'll take a few pictures to show to the director, and if he would like to shoot here, we'll present you with a contract, get a permit and work out the details."

Margie nodded. "As long as we don't have an event planned and nothing is damaged...then I don't see any problems."

A smile spread across Teresa's face. "Perfect! Well – I'll take a couple of pictures and get out of your hair."

"Shouldn't I clean up first? We had a baby shower here earlier and I haven't had time to tidy up."

Teresa shook her head. "No, that's quite all right. I just need to get an idea of how things look."

"Mom, don't we also have some pictures from weddings that were held here?"

"Oh, yes we do! I can get those to you as well."

"That would be great!"

She readied her camera, and Margie pulled Connor aside, lowering her voice. "Your friend seems very nice."

He shot her a smile. "Yes, she is. We only met yesterday – at the resort. She actually..."

He chuckled.

"What?" asked Margie. "What's so funny?"

He looked at Teresa, then back at the ground. "Well, one of the guests was yelling at me, and she told him he was being rude and told him to stop."

"Someone *yelled* at you?" Margie said.

"Yes," Connor said in a hushed voice, pressing a finger to his lips. "But it wasn't a big deal. It was just funny – she stepped in and said something. It made him mad, but it worked. He left."

Margie studied her son. His eyes were lighting up as he looked at this girl. "I like this girl."

Teresa wanted to get a few pictures of the outside of the barn, so Connor and Margie went out with her but made sure to get out of the frame. They were standing there, watching her, when Hank's car pulled up to the house. Margie waved at him and he made his way over, giving her a hug and a kiss on the cheek.

"Did I just arrive at a crime scene?" He asked. "Why is this woman taking pictures?"

Margie laughed. "No dear, it's not a crime scene. She's taking pictures for the movie!"

"Oh, of course. The movie. Okay, that explains it, see you later!" He waved at them and turned to walk toward the house.

Margie and Connor started laughing and Hank paused before making his way back to them.

"I'm sorry honey, I didn't get a chance to tell you," she said.

He laughed, shaking his head. "That's okay. It was just the way that you said it – as though it was the most normal thing in the world."

"It all happened in the last hour. That's Connor's friend, Teresa. She's working on a zombie movie and they need to have a zombie wedding – I think."

Connor shrugged. "Something like that."

They watched as Teresa took a few more pictures before rejoining them and thanking them.

"It's getting dark now," said Connor. "We can go back and catch the rest of the ghost stories. Or we could...get a bite to eat?"

Teresa's face brightened. "That'd be great! I just need to send these over to the director first."

"Sounds good to me."

Margie gave Connor a hug goodbye and watched as their cars went down the driveway.

"So," Hank said, wrapping his arms around her. "Is this all so Connor can get himself a girlfriend?"

Margie turned around and shot him a look. "*No!* She's not his girlfriend. She's just his...very pretty friend."

Hank let out a sigh. "The things we do to impress women."

"What did you do to impress me?" asked Margie, peering up at him.

"Oh, lots of things," he said, nodding. "You don't remember?"

She smiled. "I remember."

"I chopped up that tree for you."

"Oh that's right!"

"Even though I tweaked my back earlier that week and it was still a bit touchy."

"My hero." Margie gave his hand a squeeze. "Come on, I've got some dinner ready for you at home."

The next day, Hank didn't have to work so they had a lazy morning together. He made breakfast for them both and cleaned up while Margie sat outside and read a mystery novel she'd picked up at the library.

Margie was lost in the story when she thought she heard some voices – had Hank left the TV on?

"Hank?" She called out. "Is that you?"

He popped his head out of the open door. "I thought it was you talking on the phone. Hang on – it looks like someone's here."

"Oh, did I forget about a client meeting or something?" said Margie as she gathered her things and slowly stood up from her chair, bracing herself with her cane. She couldn't stand the thing, but it was better than the walker she had to use for weeks before.

She made her way around the house and saw that there were at least ten people standing around the barn.

"Can I help you?" asked Hank, a few steps ahead of Margie.

A woman with glasses turned toward him. "Hi, nice to meet you. I'm Liv, producer for *Zombies in the Sand*."

Hank shook her hand. "Uh, hello."

Margie finally caught up. "Hi Liv, I'm Margie, and this is my barn."

She smiled. "Oh it's wonderful, the director *loves* it. It's going to be a big scene in the movie – you just wait. You're going to adore it."

Margie and Hank looked at each other and then back at the woman.

A car door slammed behind them, and Margie turned around to see Teresa running toward them. "Hey guys!"

Liv held up a hand. "We don't need you here today, thanks! You need to get working on that beach – Chet wanted some more daylight shots."

"Right, of course," Teresa said, smiling. "I just – I don't think that Mrs. Clifton knew that everybody was coming today, and I just – "

"Well it's your job to inform her," Liv said before walking away.

Teresa cleared her throat. "Mrs. Clifton, I am *so* sorry, I just got word that they were coming and – "

Margie waved a hand. "Oh, it's okay. We were just a little – surprised, that's all."

Hank was standing there, arms crossed over his chest. Margie looked at him and saw the pronounced frown on his face – oh dear, he was *not* a happy camper.

"Is there anything that we need to do?" Margie asked.

Teresa shook her head. "I don't think so...let me just double check..."

Hank turned to Margie. "We're just going to let these people crawl all over the barn? What if they break something?"

"Oh don't worry so much Hank, what are they going to break, a light bulb? I'm sure it'll be fine. Let them do their thing, come on honey, help me inside."

With a huff, he agreed to walk back to the house with her. They were almost inside when they heard a voice ringing out behind them.

"Yes, just like that crippled woman! You know I never thought of the zombies moving slowly because of an impediment – but have we talked about this? Have we talked about a zombie with a cane? Where's Arnold?"

Margie stopped in her tracks. Had someone just called her a *crippled woman*?

She turned around and saw who was talking – a man with jet black hair, oversized white sunglasses and an enormous orange jacket. He looked like he was absolutely swimming in it.

"Hey you – buddy!" yelled Hank. "You will not refer to my wife as – "

Margie put up a hand to cover Hank's mouth.

"Hi there!" she yelled.

The man turned to them and smiled. "Oh, hello. Can I help you?"

Hank wrestled her hand away from his face. "Can I help *you?* You people are stomping all over my grass."

"Oh, sorry," he said, hopping off of the grass and onto a path. "I'm Chet Laret, director, *so* nice to meet you."

Margie smiled. "Nice to meet you too, Chet. I'm Margie, and this is my husband Hank."

"Chief Hank," he said, extending a hand for a handshake.

Margie knew that he was going to try to crush this man's hand, but there was nothing she could do to stop it.

Chet didn't hang on for long. "I *love* this barn. I love it! It's going to be perfect. You have a gem on your hands."

Margie beamed. "Thank you."

Hank opened his mouth to say something but Margie jabbed him in the ribs.

"Chet, is there anything that we need to do?" she asked. "Any questions that you have?"

"Right now no, but I can have someone get in touch with you if we need it," he said, nodding slowly.

"That sounds fine, we're going to go back inside," said Margie, pulling Hank toward the door.

Once Hank was safely back inside, Margie listened to two minutes of him ranting about how rude and presumptuous the entire film crew was.

"I have half a mind to arrest him for trespassing! Especially after he called you – "

"There's no need to repeat it," said Margie. "I heard him loud and clear. But at least there's one good thing to come out of all this."

Hank sighed. "What's that?"

"I might finally get to make my film debut. As a slow, limping zombie!"

Hank laughed and shook his head. "Do you know that you're something else?"

She shrugged. "That's what they tell me."

Margie didn't much care about how rude the crew was or how bizarrely the director was dressed. What interested her was how Connor looked at Teresa, and the fact that Connor couldn't hide her away now, even if he wanted to.

Chapter 6

He couldn't stop thinking about Teresa.

During his shift on Monday morning, Connor was floating in a daydream. It was fortunate that his tables weren't demanding, and he was able to get through work without any trouble.

All he could think about was his day with Teresa. They'd had *such* a wonderful time together. After taking pictures of the barn, they stopped at a local shop that served late-night cookies and snacks. They ordered a twelve inch chocolate chip brownie cookie, and devoured half of it while sitting across from each other, talking and laughing.

There was something so refreshing about her – something unusual. He'd met a lot of people during his years working around the country, and he'd made a lot of friends. There were even a few girls here and there that caught his eye, but none of them were quite like Teresa.

Most of the girls were just like him – staying in a place for only a few months at a time before looking for their next adventure.

Not that Teresa *wasn't* looking for an adventure, because she certainly was. She *drove* all the way from Ontario to pursue her dream.

He loved listening to her talk about filmmaking, though he did have to sheepishly admit to her that he'd only watched a handful of movies in the past few years; it wasn't easy to do when he spent most of his waking hours outside.

She thought that it was great, though. "That way, your tastes aren't polluted by any kind of junk," she'd said. "You're lucky actually; you've not wasted any precious time on bad movies, and now you can just watch good ones!"

"I'm all ears on recommendations." He was willing to watch anything that she wanted to show him – zombie movies, romance flicks, foreign films with subtitles. He didn't care. She pulled him in with her unyielding passion; it was so inspiring.

Maybe that was it? He met a lot of like-minded people in his travels, and that was fun. But Teresa was refreshing because she was so driven and focused – so passionate, denouncing everything in her life to go after what she wanted.

Connor had never felt that way about anything. He said yes to a lot of things, sure, so he ended up in different situations with a smattering of spontaneous fun.

That was all, though – he was used to going with the flow, not defining it.

When he got off of work, he was surprised to see that he had a missed call from Teresa. He called her back right away, but the phone only rang once before going to voicemail.

She sent him a text message a moment later. "I'm sorry – they're shooting a scene right now so I can't answer. But I'm mortified! Chet showed up at your mom's house this morning with no notice. I had no idea. I'm so sorry."

Connor frowned. He could only imagine the kind of welcome that Chief would give a bunch of strangers on his property. "I'm sure it's fine. Was she upset?"

"She wasn't, but your dad was."

"Oh, that's my stepdad – Chief Hank. His bark is worse than his bite, though. I wouldn't worry about it. Where are you guys shooting today?"

"At this house on the water near Jensen Bay. Do you want to stop by and see?"

Connor didn't have to think before answering. "Absolutely!"

Teresa sent him directions and Connor was both surprised and impressed by what he found when he got there. She was right – it did look like a legitimate movie, even if the director had claimed half of the job titles for himself.

Teresa met him over by a trailer. "Hey! It's nice to see you."

"Thanks for inviting me. I've never been on a movie set before."

She smiled. "Yeah, it's pretty exciting, isn't it? I've been kind of doubling as a production assistant today – just running around and doing whatever needs to be done."

"Well don't let me get in your way!"

"You could never be in the way," she said with a smile, a slight blush flashing on her cheeks. "I mean – it's completely fine. If anyone asks why you're here, just say you're with catering."

"Catering. A job I can do." He nodded. "So what happened at my mom's house this morning?"

"Oh gosh," Teresa rubbed her eyes. "It was terrible. Chet showed up bright and early with a bunch of people to look at the barn, and to take measurements and pictures and stuff. They wanted to get it set and dressed and everything, but they didn't tell me that they were going over there, I swear!"

"I believe you! My mom hasn't said anything about it to me, so it probably wasn't even a big deal."

Well – that was *probably* true. His mom never made a big deal about these sorts of things. There were a few things that she *did* make a big deal about, but that was usually associated with Sunday dinner or not being allowed to drive herself around. She was very excited that next week they'd be returning to her regular Sunday dinner format, instead of the potlucks that became tradition over the past few weeks.

"I still feel terrible. I'm going to stop over as soon as I can to apologize."

"I'm sure that she would – "

"Finally!" said a man about ten feet away, wrapped in a large robe. "I knew that Teresa would pull through."

Connor looked around – surely he wasn't talking to him?

Teresa stepped forward. "Hi Chet, I want you to meet Connor, he's – "

"The caterer!" Connor said quickly.

Chet frowned. "You're not my stunt double?"

Teresa and Connor exchanged glances. "Uh..."

Just then, another woman approached them. "Oh good, Teresa. I didn't know that you were working on this."

Teresa smiled and dropped her voice. "Working on what, exactly, Liv?"

"You don't know?" She lowered her voice. "Chet was supposed to film that scene of him emerging from the water. But he said it's too cold and he needs a stunt double."

"Oh, I didn't know about this."

The woman frowned. "So who is this then?"

"He's just a friend of mine. I didn't know that we needed a stunt double."

Liv sighed and shot a look over her shoulder to Chet, who was now distracted by his phone. "Then we're in trouble."

"I didn't know that he – "

Connor cleared his throat. "I can do it. I don't mind a little cold."

"You really don't have to – " Teresa started to say, but Liv cut her off.

"That's great! Let's get you dressed. Or should I say – undressed?" She winked. "We've got a spare swimsuit in one of these trailers. I'll track it down."

Teresa turned toward him, eyes wide. "You really don't have to do this. I know that the water is really cold, and I'm sure that we could find someone else to do it."

Connor shrugged. "I don't mind. It might be my only chance to be in a movie."

The woman turned around. "Are you coming?"

"Yep! Right behind you!" He said, flashing a smile at Teresa as he walked by. "I can't believe I'm finally getting my big break."

She laughed and Connor felt his spirit soar. It didn't matter how cold the water was – he'd gotten another smile out of Teresa.

The rest was icing on the cake.

Chapter 7

The knock on Amanda's car window made her jump. She'd been fully engrossed in her work and hadn't expected Margie to be done with physical therapy already.

"Sorry!" Amanda said as she rolled down the window. "That was fast! Or I guess I lost track of the time."

Margie nodded. "It was fast. But I wish you wouldn't sit out here by yourself. My physical therapist is so nice, wouldn't you prefer to come in and talk to him again?"

Amanda smiled. "I'm perfectly happy getting my work done out here in the car."

She seemed to debate that internally for a moment before saying, "Oh, all right."

Amanda was relieved that she didn't fight more. For weeks, Margie had been dropping not-so-subtle hints about how cute and kind her physical therapist was.

Amanda met the guy once, and while she didn't necessarily disagree with Margie's assessment, she just wasn't interested. She and her boyfriend Rupert broke up when she'd moved back from London, and she could hardly go an hour without thinking about calling or texting him. There wasn't room in her mind or in her heart for anyone else.

Maybe he missed her too? He said that he didn't want to do a long distance relationship, but maybe he'd changed his mind?

Amanda suspected that it was more than the distance that broke them up, though. It felt like there was something pushing them apart before her dad had his moped accident – before she even thought about moving back. Was it just an easy excuse for him? He hadn't made much effort to talk to her since she'd left...

Margie popped into the passenger seat and turned on the radio.

"How'd it go today?" asked Amanda.

"Great! I've been doing the exercises at home, as annoying as they are, and I can really see a difference."

Amanda put the car into drive. "That's wonderful."

"If only I could start driving myself around again..." said Margie with a sigh. "You have no idea what it's like to be driven around like an old woman."

Amanda laughed. "Well, I never had a car in London, so I *kind of* know how it is."

"But you had the tube!" Margie said in her best British accent. "You could take it to the pub then back to your flat."

Amanda laughed. "Have you been watching too much *Downton Abbey* again?"

"Is there such a thing as too much *Downton Abbey*?"

"No," Amanda said firmly. "I don't think there is."

Rupert had once taken her to see the real Downton Abbey – Highclere Castle. He wasn't nearly as excited about it as she was, but he went nonetheless.

When they first started dating, it was a sort of novelty to him that she was an American living in London, and that she was excited by the history, the houses and the castles. It was a novelty to her, too. She didn't quite fit in anywhere, but she thought that she would figure it out eventually.

That time never really came, though. Maybe it was her fault? She'd spent too much time with Rupert and never built a solid group of her own friends.

But she'd been in love! It was hard to think of anything else. Yet when she started missing home, Rupert made it clear that he had no intention of following her to the US.

Actually, he didn't even like traveling to the east side of the city to see her. Maybe that should have been her first sign...

"What are your plans for the rest of the day?" asked Margie.

"I think I'll just go back to the house and keep working. Nothing exciting. Unless you wanted to go somewhere else? I'm happy to drive."

Margie shook her head. "No, I don't want to be a bother."

"You're not a bother at all! I'm happy to help. Especially because Dad hardly lets me help him."

Margie chuckled. "That's not my fault. I swear he was that stubborn when I found him."

"Oh I know," Amanda said with a smile.

Her dad *was* stubborn – always had been, and always would be, it seemed. But Margie was pretty good herself.

Early on after the accident, there were times when Margie insisted that she could take care of herself, and that she absolutely did *not* want or need any help with getting dressed, or with getting in and out of the shower.

Of course, that was unsafe when her injuries were so fresh, and Amanda had to force her help onto her. Margie bickered with her, but always gave in eventually.

Amanda let her grouse without argument – she understood that it was mortifying for Margie to have to accept help and feel so vulnerable.

She was just glad that she was able to help at all; really, it gave her a chance to get to know Margie and make up, just a little bit, for how she'd behaved when they first met.

Margie was a lovely woman, and Amanda was truly happy that her dad had remarried. They were sweet together, and she hadn't seen her dad so happy in years. Probably not since before her mom's cancer diagnosis. She'd forgotten what he was like when he was happy; she forgot what *she herself* was like back then, too, when life was so much simpler...

When Amanda pulled up to the house to drop Margie off, there was a car sitting in the driveway.

"That's odd..."

"You weren't expecting any guests?"

Margie shook her head. "I don't think so."

Amanda put the car into park as they both got out, walking over to the mystery car. The door popped open and Margie's face lit up.

"Teresa! It's nice to see you again."

"Hi Mrs. Clifton."

"Please – call me Margie."

Teresa nodded. "I didn't want to be an inconvenience, but I wanted to apologize again for the film crew just showing up like that yesterday."

She pulled a bouquet of flowers from the passenger seat of her car and handed them to Margie.

"Oh my!" said Margie, accepting the flowers. "These are beautiful! But this is unnecessary – it was no trouble at all."

"No – really, it was bad. They shouldn't have dropped in like that, and I know that Chet can be a bit...unusual."

Margie waved a hand. "It was fun having a touch of Holly-wood at Saltwater Cove. Oh I'm sorry – Teresa, this is my daughter Amanda."

Amanda waved, finding herself unable to speak for a moment. Margie had never introduced her to anyone – they knew all of the same people. But she didn't even hesitate to say that she was her daughter, and not her "step" daughter. For some reason, this made her feel like something was caught in her chest.

"Nice to meet you Amanda!"

She cleared her throat. "Nice to meet you too."

"Would you like to come in? I baked a pound cake this morning and I have been hoping I'd have someone to share it with."

Amanda smiled to herself – of *course* Margie had baked something this morning.

Teresa shook her head. "No – thank you, but I need to get back to work. I just wanted to stop by and apologize again, and let you know that it does seem likely that we'll be requesting your permission to use the barn in the movie."

Margie clapped her hands together. "That's wonderful news! Just let me know what else I need to do."

"I will."

"Oh and one more thing," Margie said, holding up a finger. "Teresa, are you free on Sunday? I usually have all of the kids over for dinner, and there's always room for one of Connor's friends."

Aha. At least Amanda wasn't the only one that Margie was trying to set up with a love connection. It made her feel better – and somehow, even more like she was a real part of the family.

"That's so kind of you – I'd love to join, but we've got a night scene that we're shooting on Sunday, so I'll have to pass."

"That's too bad. Maybe next time?"

Teresa nodded. "Yes! Well, I won't hold you up any longer. Have a great day!"

"You too!" said Margie.

Once Teresa was back in her car and driving away, Amanda turned toward Margie. "So...is that Connor's girlfriend then?"

Margie smiled, admiring her flowers. "Who knows! She does seem like a sweet girl, though."

"Has Connor had a girlfriend before?"

Margie nodded. "He has. There were two that I've met – though he never seemed very serious with them. You know how he is."

Amanda nodded, though she felt a bit like an imposter. Of all of her new step-siblings, she felt like Connor was the hardest to get to know. Not that he wasn't open – because he was. He was still a guy, though, and he wasn't exactly a chatty Cathy, like Morgan.

They were all welcoming in their own way. Morgan talked her ear off and made her feel like she'd known her for years. Jade was also friendly, though not as in-your-face as Morgan.

It helped that the three of them were all living in the same house now. Her dad continued to "rent" the old house to them, and Amanda even got her old bedroom back. Jade and Morgan were great roommates; she couldn't complain.

Amanda just felt...unsure, or something. It felt like she was intruding on their lives, and it seemed like they were all doing quite well without her. Sometimes she wondered if maybe she'd be better off moving back to London once Margie was better.

But that didn't feel right either. She didn't fit there anymore, especially since all of her old friends were really Rupert's friends.

After making sure that Margie got inside safely, Amanda returned home, planning to grab a yogurt and eat lunch quickly while working on her laptop.

Her plans were thrown off, however, when she went into the kitchen and saw Morgan and Jade struggling over a cookbook.

"What're you guys making?"

"Ugh," Jade said with a groan. "We wanted to be done before you got back."

"But these cucumbers are seriously a nightmare," Morgan said, throwing a thick cucumber skin into the sink. There wasn't much of the cucumber left in Morgan's hand.

Amanda looked around, a smile creeping onto her face. "Are you making...cucumber sandwiches?"

"Yeah," Jade said with a frown. "I got this high tea cookbook because I wanted to do something to remind you of London."

"But these tiny sandwiches are harder to make than they look," Morgan said, holding up two lopsided pieces of bread.

"My scones came out perfectly though!" Jade said, beaming.

Amanda's face grew flushed. This was possibly the nicest thing that anyone had done for her in a *long* time.

She cleared her throat. "Guys this is...so sweet. It looks marvelous! Better than any tea I've seen before."

Morgan shook her head and started laughing, "It does not, and you don't have to say that."

"No really," she said, setting down her computer. "You just need an extra set of hands. Can I help?"

Chapter 8

The rest of the week really dragged on for Connor. Teresa was busy with work and she wasn't able to hang out at all; she was spending twelve, sometimes even sixteen, hours on set or scouting.

They were able to chat through text, though, which was nice. He looked forward to her messages.

"So Chet fell in love with your mom's barn, and she probably saved me from getting fired – so I owe you one! Could you do brunch on Sunday? My treat!"

Connor had to swap a shift, but he didn't mind. The most exciting part of any day was getting a message from Teresa. Sometimes she would send along pictures of what was happening on set; Connor's favorites were the zombies with their extensive makeup. They looked pretty realistic – or at least what Connor assumed a zombie might look like. He was impressed.

However, considering that Chet was the writer, director, *and* lead actor, he certainly spent a lot of time hanging around the resort. According to Teresa, he had assistant directors who "dealt with a lot of the minor (and major) details."

That was what Teresa texted Connor one evening when Chet was enjoying a relaxing dinner; meanwhile, Teresa and the rest of the crew were out in the pouring rain.

Connor snuck a picture of Chet at his private dinner feast and sent it to her.

"Ha." She'd written back. "He told us that he needed to recharge his creative battery."

"He's recharging all right," Connor replied.

"I can't say I'm surprised. And I like having you as a spy!"

Spy.

That made him laugh. Morgan would get a kick out of it too, but he didn't want to encourage her snooping.

It was the perfect set up, though. As a waiter, he was nearly invisible. And now that he knew who Chet was, he tried to take his table as often as possible, which was a battle easily won since Chet was a terrible tipper.

Best of all, Chet never seemed to recognize that Connor had played his stunt double. Maybe he would only recognize him from behind, and in swimming trunks?

That day on set had been a lot of fun for Connor. True, he had to get in and out of the water like twenty times, and by the end he couldn't hide how cold he was because his teeth were chattering – but it was still exciting.

And while Chet didn't stick around to watch him pop in and out of the water, Teresa did. She stood at the shore, never taking her eyes off of him, waiting with a towel and warm blanket.

It was better that Chet didn't recognize him, especially since Connor was always trying to hang around and overhear things that he probably shouldn't. It was very much a situation where Morgan was on his one shoulder, telling him to eavesdrop as much as possible, and Jade was on the other, telling him to stop being ridiculous.

Morgan's voice usually won.

He'd already found out some interesting information. Almost as though requested by the universe, Chet's first intriguing guest was none other than Senator Shields herself.

Connor didn't recognize her, but Kayleigh was kind enough to point her out.

"Now I see why you always volunteer to take his table," she said. "He eats with the most important people."

"What do you mean?" asked Connor.

Kayleigh nodded toward the table. "Right now, the woman he's eating with is a senator."

Connor's eyes darted between them. "Wait – do you know her name?"

"You need to take more pride in your home state Connor," Kayleigh said, poking him in the shoulder. "That's Senator Kathy Shields, of course. I wouldn't say she's a regular here, but she does come now and again. She likes to be able to have meetings while she relaxes at the resort."

Connor couldn't believe what he was hearing. "Why would a senator meet with *that* guy?"

Kayleigh shrugged. "To help him get permits? I don't know. Or maybe she wants to be a star!"

Connor did his best to snoop, but whenever he was at the table, they weren't talking about anything unusual – just the weather. What on earth was *that* about?

The next day, Chet was joined by a gaggle of people. They were all men, and unfortunately Kayleigh didn't know who any of them were. Interestingly, that was the first day that Chet ate his breakfast quickly, announcing that he needed to get back to work before scurrying off.

Connor reported this all back to Teresa, who confirmed that Chet showed up on set and started annoying everybody much earlier than expected.

"I swear," she texted, "things run much more smoothly when he's not around. Can you keep him there by promising him a frittata or something?"

Connor laughed. "I tried, but he really didn't want to stick around. Do you know any of these other people that he's been meeting with?"

"No idea. Maybe studio executives?"

"Maybe."

Connor wasn't sure what movie executives looked like, but that didn't really seem to fit. As much as Connor knew that he shouldn't generalize, two of the guys looked like they walked straight out of a mafia movie.

They were the youngest of the group – both of them dressed in tracksuits. It wasn't just the tracksuits, though – it was the big rings and gold chains that accented their outfits. He couldn't make sense of it. Were they on their way to the gym in all that activewear? Why all the jewelry, then?

They were with an older guy who did most of the talking. He had a different look – still with the gold chains, but he dressed nicer; his eyes were outlined with big, pale sunglasses that he never took off. He had tan, leathery skin and angel white hair. Connor could *maybe* buy that this guy was an executive; he acted important at least.

He never once looked at Connor, and always stopped talking when Connor came to the table. He spoke in a low voice too, so Connor could never make out what he was saying.

There were a few other guys, too. He wasn't sure which one Chet was trying to avoid the most, or who they were.

Kayleigh's information didn't help much with that, though she decided instantly that the two tracksuit guys were in the mob.

"I mean, who else would come in here dressed like that!" She put her hands on her hips. "And I'm sorry, but they've got some really thick New York accents."

Midge shot her a look. "And that's a crime? A lot of wealthy people dress like that these days. There are some women who wear yoga pants like it's their job. For all you know, they could be Silicon Valley guys."

Connor laughed. "What kind of app are those two developing?"

"Like Uber, except instead of sending a car, they send someone to break your enemy's knees?" said Kayleigh.

Whatever was going on, it gave Connor a bad feeling. Up until Chet's arrival, most of the clientele at the resort had been pretty consistent. There were the business-type people who liked having meetings in a luxury setting. He'd seen a couple of young families, obviously well-off and most interested in the tennis and guided tours. And there were the older widows, the eccentric rich men who showed up with an entourage, and the occasional minor celebrity.

But this seemed different. The more he saw of Chet's group, the more uneasy he felt. A lot of Chet's people didn't stay at the resort and only came to eat at the restaurant. And as much as Chet loved avoiding anything resembling actual work, for some reason he wanted to avoid these people even more.

As soon as they cleared out at the end of the week, Chet was back to his normal antics of taking long meals and lounging by the pool.

Though he knew that Morgan would love to hear this new information, Connor wanted to talk to Teresa about it first. When he finally got to see her at brunch on Sunday, though, he had a hard time bringing it up.

She had so many funny stories from set and pictures to show him. But finally, when he knew they were coming to the end of their time together, he forced himself to interrupt her.

"So you know how I told you that Chet seemed to be avoiding the restaurant?"

Teresa laughed. "Yeah, and he started coming to set to wreak havoc and demand last minute changes."

Connor shifted in his seat. "It's just that there was something...strange about the people he was meeting."

"What do you mean 'strange?' A lot of Hollywood people are strange. You know, they talk too loud, or too excitedly and talk over you. It can be a bit off-putting."

"Not like that. I mean at one point, he was meeting with a Washington senator."

"Oh." Teresa took the last bite of her omelette. "Weird."

Connor nodded. "I don't know what they can possibly have in common. And then there were some other people – Kayleigh is convinced that they're in the mob."

Teresa rolled her eyes. "It sounds like Kayleigh doesn't like anyone who comes through that resort."

"That might be true," Connor said with a frown. "Have you seen any of those guys? On set?"

Teresa shrugged. "I don't think so. I'm pretty sure I would know if Chet was working with the mob."

Connor laughed. "You're right. I think my sister just put ideas into my head."

"What do you mean?"

He sighed. "Well, it's a long story, but that senator was involved in a scandal on the island a few months ago."

Teresa's mouth opened. "Here? In this cute, sleepy place?"

"Yup. You wouldn't believe some of the stuff that's happened here."

She sighed. "I mean, I wouldn't put it past Chet to be involved with some sort of shady business. You've met the guy."

"Yeah."

Teresa's phone went off. "Hang on one second."

Connor sat until she was done talking to Liv.

"Sorry about that," she said, setting the phone down. "But it seems I'm needed for another crisis."

"Oh?"

Teresa nodded. "Yeah, Chet wants coffee. But not what they have there – he wants something from that Oyster Coffee place? Apparently he likes it."

Connor laughed. "Well that *is* an emergency."

Teresa had already paid the check and was gathering her things; clearly she wasn't that concerned about Chet's associates.

He cleared his throat. "Are you free at all this week? I would love to tell you more about the island scandals. There's a great taco place in Friday Harbor, maybe I could take you to dinner?"

"Oh?" She stopped what she was doing and a smile spread across her face. "Well...I know on Sunday, Chet is supposed to hold a prescreen of the movie before our night shoot. I don't know how he's going to get that all together, but I think on Saturday evening, he'll be so busy that I could sneak out."

"I think I'm working during that prescreening, actually."

Teresa groaned. "You're going to catch glimpses of a very rough cut."

"Can't wait. All right then, Saturday night it is."

"Okay!"

They both got up and went outside. Just as they were about to go back to their cars, Connor had the fleeting thought that he should give her a kiss goodbye.

But no – that would be strange and out of nowhere. It was just brunch, after all. She was just thanking him for his help in finding the barn, and he had no reason to suspect that she felt as captivated by him as he did by her.

Not yet, at least.

Chapter 9

There was a moment just before Teresa motioned to walk to her car when she thought that Connor might give her a hug goodbye, or something. But the moment passed and he just waved.

Maybe she'd imagined it?

Yeah.

Wishful thinking.

She loved spending time with him and was always sneaking onto her phone at work so that she could text him or send him pictures. Despite not being into movies, he still seemed to be interested in what she was doing.

It was...nice. Different.

Back at school, her friends were in two separate camps – the ones who were dedicated to film, and the ones who were dedicated to becoming lawyers. Each group had few interests outside of their chosen professions, and neither had much in common with the other.

Early on, she had a few disastrous parties where she tried to mingle the groups, with each group deciding that the other was boring and strange. Eventually, Teresa gave up and accepted the fact that her film friends thought she wasn't serious enough about film, and her lawyer friends thought she had an eccentric hobby that they had to pretend to humor when she brought it up.

Connor didn't fit into either of these groups. He wasn't judgy or one-dimensional; he always seemed to have a smile on his face and a willingness to listen or go along for the ride. It was, however, mortifying when Liv took advantage of his easygoing attitude and dumped him into the freezing ocean waters.

Connor didn't seem to mind – he smiled and laughed the whole time, perfectly agreeable and compliant. They had to put a wig on him to cover those glorious golden curls, but for a moment, while he stood in the frigid waters wearing only brightly colored swimming trunks, he looked *exactly* like a cool surfer dude.

When she'd first seen Connor, that's what Teresa thought he was – a cool, laid-back surfer. And now she knew that he had the abs to match that persona.

She wasn't the only one to notice; she'd overheard directions to the cameraman, bemoaning how they had to make sure not to catch too much of his muscular physique on camera, because no one would believe that it was Chet. They had to keep the shots either close up and tight or extremely far away. There were also some production assistants looking on and giggling. Connor had caused quite the stir.

Yet he didn't seem to notice. Teresa stood on the shore, feeling silly and helpless, waiting for him to be released from his dangerous task. She Googled "signs of hypothermia" and kept shouting that he needed a break to warm up. How would she explain to Mrs. Clifton that she'd turned her sweet son into a popsicle!

Mercifully, shooting didn't take long. It was only for a few seconds of film, and Connor was out and seemed healthy after not too long. Teresa rushed toward him, first draping a towel over his shoulders before taking a second towel to dry off his torso.

The only thing on her mind was getting him warmed up, though later a friend of hers scolded her for keeping all of the "ab drying responsibilities" to herself.

She also wrapped him in a warm blanket before whisking him off to a trailer to get changed. She was trying to keep it professional – she was just trying to be a good assistant and do whatever was needed. In that way, she did a good job.

Yet now she was mentally back in that moment, seeing him in her mind's eye, wondering if Connor had ever tried surfing. She knew that he kayaked, mountain biked, skydived...

Her phone went off and brought her back to reality. She had five text messages from Liv. Chet changed his mind on his coffee order – he wanted the nondairy whipped topping, the real stuff was making him gassy, apparently.

She let out a sigh and got into her car before responding. "I'm on it."

Once she had the requested coffee, she headed straight over to set. The past few days had been a bit less hectic because they were shooting in an old warehouse where they'd built a few indoor sets. It was easier to not have to worry about the weather and other factors, but it also meant that Chet felt no restraints in calling for endless takes and retakes.

It was never his own scenes that he wanted to reshoot – those looked fine to him on playback. But he'd want the other actors to speak a certain way, or to move the way he'd envisioned it. Teresa could see the annoyance on their faces, but Chet seemed impervious to it.

Someone had to have a vision, though, and that someone was Chet. At least he seemed sure of his opinions. That had to be a good thing, right?

Chet was now fixated on a seemingly unimportant scene – one where his roommates in the movie were making breakfast before deciding to go out into zombie-infested territory.

"This is their last moment of freedom," Chet kept stressing. "Is *that* how you'd crack an egg if it was your last moment of freedom?"

Teresa wasn't sure if she agreed with him; how would the roommates know that it was going to be their last breakfast before they turned into zombies? They weren't psychic, unless Chet had done another rewrite.

But it wasn't her place to say anything. Instead, after chatting with the wardrobe girls for a while, she wandered over to the catering table to see if there were any healthy options for snacks.

Predictably, there weren't, and she quickly gave into an enticing donut instead.

As she ate the donut, she was focused on typing out a long message to Connor about the coffee shenanigans when some loud voices caught her attention. She turned around and saw two people that she didn't recognize at the other end of the catering table.

"I never said I wasn't gonna do it," the one man said to the other.

"Go ahead and do it! No one's stopping you."

Teresa looked around – the men were attracting glares from the rest of the crew. A text popped up on Teresa's phone from Liv. "Tell those two to keep it down."

Great.

Teresa let out a sigh and walked over to them. "Excuse me?"

They didn't notice her at first; she had to clear her throat and repeat herself, louder this time. "Excuse me, gentlemen?"

One of the men turned around and looked her over from top to bottom. "Why *hello* there."

Teresa reminded herself not to flinch or cross her arms at his examination. "Can I help you? Are you guys looking for someone?"

"No thanks, we're fine," said the other.

They seemed like they were about to ignore her again, so Teresa spoke up. "Well, we're filming here guys, so I have to ask you to keep your voices down. Or better yet – you can take it outside."

"Oh, do you want to come outside with us?"

Ew.

"I'm sorry, who are you with again?" she said, setting a firm tone to her voice.

"We're with Chet. You could say that he considers us some of his closest friends."

"I see. Maybe I could show you somewhere else where you can sit down and be more comfortable – "

"We're comfortable here. We need to see what's going on."

Teresa shifted her weight. She wasn't sure what else to tell them. "Okay..."

"But maybe you can show us around," said the one, gently brushing her arm.

Teresa pulled away. "Just remember to keep your voices low."

She walked off, texting Liv that she didn't know who those guys were, but they claimed to be Chet's friends.

"Do we need to get security?" Teresa asked.

Liv's response was immediate. "Absolutely not. And don't make them angry."

Well *that* wasn't alarming or anything. She couldn't help it now, Connor's words were ringing in her head. He'd decided that Chet was working with the mob, and now she couldn't help but think of it too.

Those two certainly didn't look like someone that Chet would *actually* be friends with. She couldn't really imagine Chet having any friends at all, though, so who knew?

It was all a bit odd. And investors for movies like this came in all shapes and sizes. Who was she to judge if this was the company that Chet kept? He was the one who was paying her to be here, after all.

Or at least, she was supposed to get paid soon. There were some issues in accounting, but Teresa didn't want to ask questions. Maybe those guys were with accounting?

Okay, *that* was a stretch. She managed to snap a picture of them and sent it to Connor. "Are these the guys you saw at breakfast the other day? They told me that they're Chet's friends."

Connor didn't write back for almost ten minutes – he must've been busy. "Yeah – that's them! Those are Kayleigh's mob guys."

Teresa groaned and answered him. "I'm sure that they're not in the mob."

It couldn't be. It made no sense. That was something you saw *in* the movies – not on movie *sets*. She had to stop standing around, thinking up conspiracy theories. She needed to get back to work.

But the guys had a different idea. The pushier one approached her.

"So what does a pretty woman like yourself do around here?"

"Uh – a little bit of everything, I guess."

"Oh yeah? That's good, that's good."

Teresa needed to be in control of this conversation. "What do you do?"

He smiled, rubbing his hands together. "I'm in real estate. It's a very successful business, you know."

She broke eye contact, acting like she needed to read something on her phone. "Sure."

"So when do you get off the clock? I was thinking maybe you could show me around the island."

"That's really up to Chet – we have a lot left to do here and – "

"Chet!" The man's voice boomed across the set. "Come over here."

Teresa stood, eyes wide as Chet obediently appeared before them.

"What's up man?"

"I've been talking to your very beautiful associate here, and I think you're overworking her."

Teresa shook her head. "No – I'm not overworked. I'm very happy."

"She's being modest. I think I need to take her out on the town for a while."

Teresa froze. She was happy to do whatever Chet asked her to do – whether it was going back to the same location ten times or bringing him overly complicated coffee. But she was *not* going to be handed off like some farm animal.

Chet's eyes darted between them. "Sorry Lenny, but I need her to show me some of the new locations today."

"Aw come on man, can't it wait?"

"No," Chet said firmly. "Not if we want this movie to finish on schedule. Excuse us, guys."

Teresa took her cue and followed Chet. Neither of them turned around when Lenny yelled behind them, "Say hi to your dad for us, Chet!"

When they got outside and a good distance away from the building, Chet stopped and turned toward her.

"Teresa, you need to be careful around those guys."

Her eyes widened. "Why? I mean – who are they?"

"They're just – friends of a friend." He sighed. "You know how it is, it takes all kinds to make a movie."

Teresa nodded, though she had no idea what he was talking about. She'd never seen him like this before – he was usually overly grand and jolly, laughing or talking loudly. Now his eyes were darting around, looking behind Teresa and checking the parking lot.

She cleared her throat. "Did you want to see those beaches again?"

"That's a good idea," he said. "I think for a while, you should hang close to me. Okay?"

She didn't like serious Chet. "Okay."

"I'm just going to let Liv know that we're going to step out for a while – I'm sure they can handle it. That scene is as good as it's going to get."

Teresa just nodded and smiled. As she waited for Chet to finish talking to Liv, she pulled out her phone and saw that she had a message from Connor. "Yeah, I'm sure you're right. We just get bored at work and have overactive imaginations."

Chet turned around. "Are you ready to go?"

"Yep!" She said, dropping her phone into her purse and getting the keys to her car.

Maybe Connor was onto something, and maybe he wasn't. No matter what was going on with those guys, she couldn't let it affect her. Teresa needed to focus on doing her job and doing it well – that was all that she could think about for now.

Chapter 10

"Mom, I can't believe that you used to do a huge meal like this every Sunday," Connor called out as he set the table.

"Not *every* Sunday – just most Sundays. And not everyone could make it to every dinner. But it was always an option! Last year for your sister's birthday, we had everyone here except for you. So this birthday is even better."

Connor smiled. It was like his mom's greatest wish was to have them all at the same place at the same time.

How many of these dinners had he missed? He was glad, at least, that he was here for this one. And that he could help his mom – because as much as she didn't want to admit it, she still wasn't back to full speed.

Amanda came over early too, excited to be a part of the famous Sunday dinners. As they were setting up a makeshift bar on a side table, Amanda mentioned that she'd gotten to meet Teresa.

"Really? Where?"

She smiled. "She stopped by to give your mom apology flowers."

"Oh yeah. I heard about that from my mom. That was nice of her."

"It was. Then your mom invited her to tonight's dinner..."

Connor laughed. "Now *that* I didn't hear about."

"Unfortunately, she couldn't make it. Or...do you prefer that she's not here?"

Connor set down a wine glass. "What do you mean?"

Amanda shrugged. "I just wasn't sure if you liked Teresa. I mean, I'm not sure that your mom didn't also invite her physical therapist to dinner in some attempt to get me to hit on him."

"Oh," Connor said with a laugh. "Sorry about that. She does that to everyone."

"It's okay. I just wasn't sure if Teresa was the same sort of situation for you."

Connor kept his eyes fixed on the table in front of him as he straightened everything out. "No...I wouldn't say that."

Amanda smiled but said nothing more. She didn't mention anything during dinner, either, which Connor was thankful for.

Not that he was embarrassed of how he felt about Teresa or anything, but it was so new. If it got out into the open, he could only imagine what kind of questions Morgan would have, what jokes Luke or Matthew might crack, and heaven forbid the sort of ideas that his mom would get.

Connor didn't manage to bring up any topics during dinner, because it was wonderfully chaotic. With everyone around the table, there were multiple conversations going on at once.

Tiffany was talking about her new business with Sydney, while Jade was telling everyone about developments with the park. Morgan and Luke were teasing each other, as they often did; Matthew had stories from recent arrests and Hank weighed in with his opinions.

Connor could hardly get a word in edge wise – not that he needed to. He was happy to sit back and watch the chaos unfold.

He wasn't planning to talk about the movie until Morgan prompted him.

"Have you guys heard about the zombies on San Juan Island?" Morgan said after everyone was mostly finished eating.

Tiffany cocked her head to the side. "Should I be concerned?"

"No," Connor said, finally speaking up. "They're shooting a movie here, and I have a friend on the crew."

"That's really interesting," said Sydney. "I wonder what made them choose the island for filming – I can't imagine it's very cost-effective."

Connor frowned. "I'm not sure, actually. I know it's supposed to be about a zombie attack on an island."

"Yeah..." said Jade slowly. "You'd think that they could just film it anywhere and make it *look* like an island."

"Are we even sure that this is a *real* movie?" Morgan said as she crossed her arms.

"What's this?" asked Matthew.

Jade rolled her eyes. "It's just Morgan's screwy theory. She insists that there must be some sort of scandal on the island."

"Actually...she might be right. Or she's gotten into my head now, too."

Morgan's eyes brightened. "Really? So you believe me? What did you unearth!"

Connor sat back. Everyone was looking at him now. Maybe he shouldn't say anything? But Teresa didn't seem to think it was a big deal. "Well first of all, the movie director keeps interesting company."

"Interesting? What does that mean?" asked Morgan.

Luke placed a hand on her shoulder. "I think, my dear, Connor is talking about the zombies. Misunderstood creatures."

Morgan shot him a look and Connor suppressed a laugh before continuing. "Not exactly. But the director, Chet, met with a certain senator last week."

Morgan gasped. "I *knew* it! I knew she wasn't done with us!"

"Are you serious, Connor?" asked Jade.

He nodded. "I swear. One of my coworkers recognized her. They only met for lunch – but it still seemed strange."

Jade frowned. "Matthew, have you heard anything about the senator getting in trouble again, or getting involved with other stuff?"

"No, I don't think so. Have you, Chief?"

He laughed. "I hear all kinds of stuff."

"And you didn't tell us!" Morgan threw down her napkin, incredulous.

"You never asked," Chief said with a shrug. "There's nothing officially on the books about Senator Shields. Let's just say she seems to have a pattern of unscrupulous behavior. And crooks run in packs."

"Yeah, but what *kind* of unscrupulous behavior?" urged Morgan. "Did she fall in love with another much younger man?"

Luke lifted his eyebrows. "Connor? Is it you? Did she sweep you off your feet?"

"Absolutely not, Luke," Connor said with a laugh. "Like I said, it was only one meal. And then she was gone."

Morgan sat back, her stare fixed on him. "Is there anyone else that you've neglected to tell us about, Connor?"

All eyes on him again. Maybe it wasn't a good idea to tell everyone his theories. But at the same time, he had nothing else interesting to share.

"Maybe."

Amanda giggled but said nothing. Connor realized that he couldn't remember her speaking once during the entire dinner. Maybe she felt left out?

"I don't want to weave a Morgan-style tale here," said Connor. "My friend Teresa is working on the movie. Amanda, you met her, she's nice right?"

Amanda nodded. "Yeah, she seems nice. Do you think that she knows the senator?"

Connor shook his head. "No. She had no idea about why the director would meet with her. And she also didn't know the two mob-looking guys who met with Chet either."

Morgan slapped her hands on the table. "Did you hear that! What did I tell you."

"Yeah, that's the thing!" Connor said. "You put that idea in my head, and I convinced myself that these guys were trouble. And I was stupid enough to bring it up to Teresa!"

"Connor!" Jade said.

His mom had a similar disapproving look on her face. "You can't just go accusing people of being involved with the mafia. Right Hank?"

"I mean, *I* can," Chief said with a smile. "But yeah, the rest of you shouldn't."

"Did they offer you protection?" asked Morgan. "More importantly – did you accept it?"

"They did. And of course."

"Ew, don't joke about that," said Tiffany. "It's not like that in real life."

"How do you know?" asked Morgan.

"Actually," Sydney interjected, "It *can* be like that. Not that I've ever had to deal with it personally, but my uncle has not always been so lucky. He says it was much worse in the eighties, though."

"Okay, thank you very much Morgan for putting this idea into everyone's heads," said Jade. "I'd like to get back to the more important issue at hand: Tiffany's birthday."

Tiffany sighed. "You really don't have to."

Connor's mom stood up, clapping her hands together. "Oh, I think we do!"

After cake and presents, they retired to the living room to play a game of charades. Sadly, Morgan's suggestion of duck-duck-goose was rejected by the birthday girl. Connor would've liked to see Chief playing the goose.

There was no more talk of the mob and thankfully, no more questions about Teresa either. Connor couldn't help but wonder how the evening would've gone if Teresa had been able to accept his mom's invitation. Would she have found them all too intimidating? Or crazy?

Maybe she would have enjoyed everyone's company? She said that she was looking for friends on the island. She probably would like everyone – as long as Morgan didn't scare her off right away. Maybe when she had more free time they could all meet...

Though Connor had just heard that the prescreen had been postponed until next week, so that probably meant that Teresa would be busier than ever. And maybe, since he really liked Teresa, it'd be better to keep her away from his family and their theories as long as possible.

He hoped that she wouldn't cancel their plans on Saturday. Connor was determined to see her and treat her to a nice dinner – even if he had to sneak onto set in those swim trunks again.

Chapter 11

After Amanda finished her presentation at the Seattle office on Thursday, she decided to reward herself by taking a few hours off of work to relax back on the island at Fourth of July beach.

The project she'd been working on with her team had taken longer than expected, but the client was thrilled with the results and Amanda felt like she'd earned a break after working so many late evenings. Overall, her transfer to the Seattle office seemed to create more work than ever – sometimes she felt the need to make up for the fact that she wasn't living in the city. Hopefully things could calm down now that this big project was finished.

While she was waiting to drive off of the ferry and into Friday Harbor, she scrolled through old pictures on her phone and stumbled across an album from two years prior. It was from her trip to Dublin with Rupert.

She must've taken a hundred pictures on that trip – everything from him grabbing a beer in the pub, to dinner on the evening they arrived, to a slew of selfies that she insisted on taking with him.

She let out a sigh. They'd been so happy then – what happened?

Last Thursday, she'd had a weak moment where she texted him to see how he was doing. He responded civilly, saying that he was doing well and he hoped that she was too, but added,

"Though if you're reaching out I can only assume things are not going well for you."

She'd suspected that he had a new girlfriend, but this cold text confirmed it. That response didn't even sound like him – it sounded like someone else had carefully crafted it for him.

Probably this new girl, wishing that Amanda would disappear and stop contacting her beau. Amanda couldn't blame her – she would've felt the same way.

But it still hurt.

She got the okay to drive off of the ferry and headed straight for Fourth of July Beach. It was always one of her favorite spots when she was growing up. They used to go there during high school and have picnics and late-night dance parties on the sand. All of her friends had moved away, though, and the traditions left with them.

She was surprised to find all of the parking spots taken; she had to park a bit down the road. She didn't mind, though – she welcomed the walk.

Once the beach was in sight, Amanda finally understood why there were so many visitors – an eerie number of people on the beach looked like zombies.

Whoops!

She turned around and headed back up the trail to the road. She was looking down at her feet, walking quickly, when she ran into someone.

"Oh my gosh, I'm sorry!" she said.

The man stopped and looked her up and down. "Oh, hello! Have we met before?"

"Uh – I don't think so."

"Are you my new talent?"

"No..." Amanda looked over her shoulder, wondering if she was about to get in trouble when she saw that Teresa was a few feet behind the man.

"Hey!" Teresa called out. "Chet, this is my friend Amanda."

He stuck out a hand. "How do you do? I'm Chet Laret, director of *Zombies in the Sand*."

"Oh," said Amanda. "I've heard so much about you."

"Thank you," he said, smiling broadly. "It's been quite a whirlwind. I can't believe that Teresa didn't tell me about her *adorable* actress friend!"

"I'm not an actress," Amanda said firmly. "Nor do I have any interest in being one."

He raised his eyebrows. "Well not with *that* attitude! But I can't pretend to not understand, I have the same sort of love-hate relationship with my career. There's just so much to it, right down to how you decide to present yourself every day, don't you agree?"

Amanda stared at him. Was that a dig at her? Or did it have something to do with how he was presenting himself to the world – in yellow parachute pants? "Uh huh."

"I know!" He threw his hands up. "It was very nice meeting you, but I must get back to set."

"Nice...meeting you too?"

Teresa and Amanda watched as Chet hurried off, his long legs swiftly putting a distance between them.

"Well that was bizarre," Amanda said, turning to Teresa.

"I'm sorry. He's in a really manic mood right now."

"Do you just have to follow him around all day?"

Teresa shrugged. "Something like that. Today's been great, though. This beach is perfect! We started shooting on South

Beach yesterday, and it was so windy that we had to move over here. This has been way better."

Amanda nodded. "Yeah, that'll happen on South Beach."

"It's much quieter. We've hardly seen anyone except for a few dog walkers and one very social golden retriever who wandered onto set. And you! I guess."

Amanda laughed. "Yeah, sorry about that. I almost walked right into it. I just wanted to take a break from work and walk along the water."

"Sorry we're in the way. We'll be out of here soon enough." Teresa clasped her hands together. "Would you like to come anyway? Just to see how everything works?"

Amanda looked around. "Really?"

"Yeah! There have to be *some* perks to being Chet's right-hand man – I'm sorry, right-hand woman."

Amanda smiled. "Sure."

They headed toward the beach and Teresa showed Amanda around, introducing her to different groups.

"Sometimes it feels like I'm at a weird, dysfunctional summer camp," Teresa told her. "It's a lot of fun, though."

"Is it a stressful job?"

Teresa shrugged. "Sometimes. It's not too bad, though."

"Do you get yelled at a lot?"

Teresa laughed. "I mean, not really. There are some tense moments, but overall most people aren't jerks."

"Huh." Amanda took a look around. Everyone seemed busy now – there was no yelling, just a lot of activity.

"Why, do you get yelled at a lot at your job?"

Amanda nodded. "Oh yeah. All the time."

Teresa stopped walking and pulled back. "Wait, really? Don't you work in an office? I know that movies have a reputation for abusing their staff but it's not normal and – "

"Yeah, it's really just my boss. She has these ideas and then gets really upset and throws things."

"Amanda, that sounds *horrible*. You shouldn't have to put up with that."

"I didn't see much of it when I was working in London," Amanda said with a sigh. "And now I work from home a lot, so the most she can do is call me up and yell at me. But any time I see her, it's a wild card."

"You should look for another job! Apparently Chet is ready to hire you on as an actress."

"That was the ego boost I needed today," Amanda said with a laugh. "Though it's probably just this outfit. I had to get dressed up to present to a client today."

She stopped, noticing two guys hovering near them, whispering to each other.

"Do you know them?"

"Sort of," Teresa said. "Uh – maybe we should go find Chet and – "

It was too late. Amanda's eye contact was an apparent invitation to one of the men.

"Please tell me that you're not going to let them ruin your beautiful face with zombie scars," he yelled over.

"Maybe you could ask them to do something to help your face," Amanda yelled back.

Teresa shot her a look. "*Amanda!*"

"Oh – I'm sorry," she responded in a lowered voice. "Is he like, the star or something?"

"Not exactly..."

He walked over, a half smile on his face. "Are you new around here?"

She didn't know why Teresa was reacting to this guy like this – he looked like a goober. Amanda stared at him, letting the silence hang between them until he looked like he was about to speak again. "No," she said flatly.

He put his hands up. "All right, all right! If that's how you're going to be."

Amanda continued staring at him until he turned around and returned to his friend.

Teresa grabbed her arm and pulled her away. "How did you do that!"

"Do what?"

"Get him to leave you alone." She motioned behind her. "Those are the guys that Connor has a...you know...*theory* about."

Amanda narrowed her eyes. "Wait, really? What do they do all day?"

"Mostly just hang around and try to hit on everyone."

Amanda nodded. "Oh, I see. Yeah, men don't usually try to flirt with me. I think it has to do with my sunny personality – I get it from my dad."

Teresa laughed. "I'm so impressed."

"So they just stand around and leer at you?"

Teresa shrugged. "I mean, just some days. And Chet usually keeps me close to him so they leave me alone."

Amanda looked around to make sure the guys weren't nearby. "Isn't that a little strange, Teresa? That he has to protect you from these weird dudes on his own set?"

"They're just his friends I guess." She paused, staring at a trailer in the distance. "Oh – let me see if the makeup girls can give you a zombie bite!"

"Okay," Amanda said, forcing a smile.

She spent about twenty more minutes on set before deciding that it was time to go. When she got back to her car, she pulled out her phone and called Connor.

"Hey, what's up?"

"Hey, do you have a minute to talk?"

"Sure – my battery is low, though. Fair warning that I could drop off at any moment."

Amanda laughed; she admired Connor's carefree attitude and wished she could be more like him sometimes. But she also wished that he would learn to charge his phone. "I just had a very weird interaction on the set of the zombie movie."

"Did they come for your *brains!*"

"Ha, very funny." Amanda started the engine – she might need to make an escape if that dude came looking for her again. "No. I ran into Teresa and she invited me to look around, which was really nice."

"But?"

"But...those guys were hanging around set and it was a really weird vibe. Do you have a picture of them?"

"Sort of. Teresa sent me one once, but it's not the greatest quality. Why?"

"Well...isn't your Uncle Mike in the FBI?"

Connor laughed. "Who told you that?"

"My dad. What, am I not supposed to know?"

"It's nothing like that..." Connor said. "It's just that we don't really talk about it."

"Why not?"

"Just, you know..." Connor sighed. "One of those things."

Amanda wasn't going to push him – it didn't matter. "Well, can we give him the picture of the guys to look into? I mean I could ask my dad, but he'd probably just say no."

Connor laughed. "Better you asking than me. And I can try sending it to my uncle but...I don't know, do you really think that's a good idea?"

Amanda bit her lip. "According to Teresa, the guys just hang around and annoy everyone."

"What do you mean?"

"I mean that Teresa has to stay near Chet so that they don't...harass her."

Connor was silent for a moment. "You mean they're just..."

"Yeah."

"Well then." He cleared his throat. "I'll send this over to my uncle right away, and can you try asking your dad too?"

Amanda smiled. "Deal."

Chapter 12

The rescheduled movie screening put considerable strain on the staff at Whispering Waves Resort. Connor was the only one eager to volunteer his help; he didn't want to miss his chance to be around Chet and his "friends" for any reason.

They set up a private banquet room in the resort early Friday morning. Connor worked his regular shift at the restaurant before reporting there to help.

Unfortunately, Teresa wasn't invited to the screening. She wouldn't be able to casually sneak in, either – they were told that they had to prevent any other guests from wandering toward the banquet hall and that Chet would have security standing at the doors. He said it was vital that the movie wasn't leaked to the public early.

Who on *earth* was anticipating this movie, though? Connor couldn't figure it out. He went online and did a search – there was no buzz about it whatsoever. Nothing on the film websites, or even on zombie message boards. What kind of fantasy world did Chet live in?

It didn't matter, and he didn't mention any of it to Teresa. She had to go to Seattle anyway to help with one of the actress's boyfriends. Apparently, the actress threw a tantrum about how she couldn't work without more support, and Chet agreed to have her boyfriend flown in from Los Angeles.

If Connor weren't already used to diva behavior, he would've thought this was very strange. But Teresa assured him it was nothing out of the ordinary and that she was happy to do it – though she did stress that she couldn't wait to hear how the screening went.

"Tell me if you hear my name dropped!" she wrote in a text.

A moment later, she texted again. "Actually – I don't want to know. Good or bad – you shouldn't feel like you have to eavesdrop on my behalf. And it's wrong. I know better."

"Just know," he wrote back, "that if anyone says anything bad about you, I will spill soup on them, and I will make it look like an accident."

"You're the best. If it comes to that...take pics!"

Connor was tasked with serving appetizers – the perfect job for someone who wanted to eavesdrop. The first people to arrive were three guys Connor had never seen before, and they spent about an hour setting up the screen and making sure that the video was loaded.

Connor offered them some refreshments, but they declined, saying that they were there to make sure things ran smoothly.

Next to arrive was Liv. Concerned that she might recognize him, Connor went back to the kitchen and pretended to organize some of the platters. When he returned half an hour later, Liv was gone and the room had filled out considerably.

It was a small place, and with about forty attendees, nearly every seat would be filled. Connor resumed his appetizer responsibilities, taking time to slowly work his way toward Chet, who was surrounded by a group of people.

"What we're doing here is redefining the genre," Chet said, a glass of champagne in one hand and a stuffed mushroom in the other. "I've got a great team and that doesn't come cheap, you know?"

The people surrounding him seemed to be in agreement, nodding and expressing words of support. Connor slowly went to each of them, offering them the tiny vegetable kebabs on his platter, but nearly everyone waved him away. He'd need to have a better appetizer if he wanted any sort of lingering time.

He listened as long as he could, but none of the other people were talking – it was all Chet, and everything that came out of his mouth sounded like blustering. After a few minutes, Connor grew bored of the zombie trope conversation and left the area.

Okay, so maybe he'd gone to the wrong group. They seemed to be actual film nerds – or Chet toadies.

He went back to the kitchen and dropped off the platter; it was still full, but no one wanted vegetables anyway. He saw that there was a new tray of fried cheese balls.

Perfect.

Now *that* was what he needed to be able to hang around the mob guys.

Connor returned to the room, relieved to see that people were still mingling. He wasn't sure what time the movie was supposed to start, and he wanted to get as much time as he could inside that room while people were still talking.

He spotted the group of mob guys – the two he'd seen from before, their older buddy, and a handful of other serious looking men. He took a deep breath and walked over.

"Fried mozzarella?" he said, offering the tray to tracksuit number one.

He grunted. "Finally! Something I can eat."

Connor smiled and offered him a napkin.

"I'm telling you, the prices are through the roof around here. That building I showed you – if we hang onto that for a year, maybe two? We can clear a few million, easy. But we can't keep it too long – not so long that anyone notices – and then we pass it off to Benzini."

"I like this. I like this a lot," the older man said before turning to look at Connor. "My friend, you need to back up."

Connor cleared his throat. "Sorry, I'm just trying to get rid of all of this cheese – nobody else wants it."

"Oh, I can help you with that," said tracksuit number two, as he shoved the rest of the cheese balls onto his plate.

Connor smiled. "Thanks."

Dang it. Just as he was starting to hear something interesting, the older guy got wise. He went back to the kitchen, desperate for something else that the guys might like. There was nothing.

"Hey, what's going on? I need to grab another tray."

Midge shook her head. "We're supposed to stop for now, they're going to screen the movie. And then we'll pick up after."

Connor frowned. "Should I bring around a tray of champagne or something?"

"He wouldn't pay for champagne for his guests," Midge said with a laugh. "You'd be better off with a pitcher of water."

Connor knew that she was joking about the water, but it wasn't a bad idea. He grabbed a pitcher from the fridge and headed back to the room.

Everyone was in their seats and Chet was at the front of the room, giving an impassioned speech that Connor had no interest in. Instead, he carefully watched the different groups that he'd identified earlier in the evening.

The artsy people stuck together, close to the front, where Chet stood. There was another group of bored looking people scattered through the middle of the room. Connor couldn't find any unifying characteristics for this group. And the mob guys were all bunched together in the far corner.

Connor decided to park himself behind them with his pitcher of water. Luckily they were by a table, where he could quietly fill water glasses as he tried to listen in.

The guys made a few snide remarks and laughed throughout Chet's speech, but it was nothing substantial – at least not that Connor could make out. It sounded like they were just making fun of him.

After an agonizing half hour of Chet speaking, the movie started to play. Connor was horrified to see that it opened with a shot of *him*.

He looked around the room nervously – everyone was still looking forward, focused on the screen. It was only from behind, and he was essentially unrecognizable, but still! Not good for this sort of mission.

Thankfully, it cut away from that scene quickly, but it was all downhill from there. What followed was a seemingly random collection of zombie attack scenes, Chet's character having arguments with people, and finally, a boat riding off into the distance.

Connor couldn't make heads or tails of what he had just witnessed, and as the lights went back up, he saw the same look of confusion on the rest of the attendees' faces.

Chet cleared his throat and got back to the front of the room. "Like I said, this film is still very much a work in progress and we're several weeks away from getting all of the footage that we need to complete it. I thank you all for coming and I look forward to chatting with you this evening."

The mob group broke into murmurs and Connor quickly busied himself with filling up water glasses and arranging them on trays.

"Listen, I don't care what this kid says – we're not giving him another dime."

Tracksuit number one let out a groan. "How are we supposed to keep him happy then?"

"You know," said tracksuit number two, "all I ever see is people standing around, not doing anything. Why do they need to be paid anyway?"

The older guy waved his hand. "I don't care. We've done what we promised, and we don't need to do any more. You understand? Get that through to him."

Connor was just turning around, holding a tray of water when the old man walked toward him. He made sure to step out of the way – otherwise he would've been knocked over.

So whoever they were, they *were* paying for this monstrosity of a movie – though they were not going to give Chet another dime, apparently.

Connor walked around, offering the waters to each group, and being mostly refused by all. The artsy looking people surrounded Chet again, telling him how revolutionary the movie was and how realistic looking the zombies were.

"I mean I *know*, it's so important to get that right. I flew my makeup artists in from LA, and I had to pay them double their normal rate to pull them away from another job. It's been a nightmare – a real nightmare!"

"Well. *Obviously* it's worth it," said one of the women. "I know this was just a sneak peek, but it's phenomenal Chet!"

Chet sighed. "It's just the beginning. Excuse me while I try and talk some sense into my investors."

"Good luck!"

Forget the waters, Connor needed something good. He set his tray on a nearby table and returned to the kitchen.

"Midge! What do we have?"

She sighed. "Not much, to be honest. We could dress up some garlic bread? Make it look fancy?"

"Perfect."

Armed with a new tray of appetizers, Connor returned and zeroed in on Chet's new group.

"I'm telling you, sometimes costs go up while filming. It's not unexpected. We have to keep talent happy, and that costs money."

A woman in the group crossed her arms. "How much, Chet? I came here to see your numbers, not to watch some thrown together attempt at a trailer."

"At this point, a million would do it. I've been holding off on paying the staff – "

"Just a million?" She snickered. "Let's get real."

Chet continued. "I don't want to have to break the news to them that they're not going to get paid."

"I don't understand how this even became an issue," she said. "What you should have been doing – "

"I'm doing everything I need to be doing," said Chet firmly. "And I know that my dad wants this to be seen through to the end."

Connor had finally made his way around the circle and only had Chet left to serve.

He cleaned his throat. "Garlic bread, sir?"

Chet waved him off without even looking at him.

Connor had to walk away before he could hear the rest of their conversation. He was plotting his next move when he heard a crash at the other end of the room.

Kayleigh was on her hands and knees, looking like she was on the brink of tears. Connor rushed over to her.

"Are you okay?" he asked, kneeling beside her. "Hey, it's all right, we'll get this cleaned up."

"It wasn't my fault, someone bumped into me. Look at all of this glass," she said, her voice cracking.

"It's fine! Oh man – you shouldn't pick that up with your hands. You're bleeding."

She looked down at her hand before throwing a rag across the room.

Connor set his tray on a nearby table. His snooping would have to wait. "It's okay, don't get upset. Go to the bathroom – get that washed off and bandaged. I'll clean this up."

She reached out and touched his shoulder. "Thanks, Connor. You're always looking out for me."

"Just being a good coworker," he said, smiling up at her.

Tears welled up in her eyes again.

"What's wrong?" he asked. "It's really not a big deal."

She stared at him for a moment. "Is that all?"

"Uh – is what all?"

She sighed and without another word, stood and rushed out of the room.

Connor wasn't sure what had made her *so* upset – she seemed to take this job too seriously, it was just a bit of broken glass. He spent the next twenty minutes cleaning up and unfortunately, by the time he was finished, nearly everyone had left except for Chet.

When Connor was just about done, Liv returned to talk to Chet; Connor made sure to keep his head down.

"How'd it go?" she asked.

"Terrible," said Chet. "The clip was awful. Who did that? They're fired."

Liv sighed. "So I guess we're not getting any more money."

"Listen – has the crew caught on to anything?"

"Not really. Grumblings here and there, but I keep telling them that accounting made a mess of payroll."

"Good. But we need to speed up production – maybe we can compress it into seven weeks?"

"Do you really think that anyone is going to work without pay for that long?"

"That's your job to figure out. My job is to make this movie happen."

With that, Chet left the room.

Liv let out a sigh before pulling out her phone. As she passed by Connor, she looked down and said, "Ugh. Bosses, am I right?"

"Yeah," Connor responded without lifting his head.

She walked out, leaving Connor with the bag of broken glass and the mess of his broken thoughts.

Chapter 13

Despite Chet being in a sour mood, the rest of the week's filming went well. Teresa spent almost fourteen hours on set on Saturday, but it didn't bother her. The assistant director said he was impressed with her "hustle," plus she had something to look forward to – her dinner with Connor!

For the entire week, as they texted and chatted back and forth, Teresa debated if Connor was just being friendly, or if this dinner was more like a date. Ultimately, she decided that there was no way to be sure unless she came out and told him how she felt.

It was a bold move. But with work going so well, and all of the friends and connections she'd made on the crew, it felt like she'd never been more lucky. If there was ever a time to take a chance, it was now.

Connor offered to pick her up, but then realized it might get him in trouble at the resort, so instead Teresa said she'd come to get him.

"I don't know if you're ready to see the shack that I'm living in," he said.

"It can't be that bad."

"It's better than the tent I stayed in for a month. Except the tent had nicer views."

She wasn't sure if he was kidding about that, but knowing Connor – probably not. After some cajoling, he sent over his address.

She had just enough time to get home, shower, and throw on a dress before going to get him. His place wasn't far; she followed his directions and found the long, winding driveway that weaved through the property. It felt like she rode along it for a half mile before she reached the end – a clearing with several cabins and trailers.

It didn't look *bad* – it was just...secluded. Sure, some of the trailers were decked out in Christmas decorations, and the cabins had overgrown brush and grass around them. But some of the grass seemed to have wildflowers speckled throughout, so if she squinted, she could imagine that it was almost roman-tic-looking.

Connor popped out of his cabin before jumping into her passenger seat.

"Thanks for picking me up!" he said. "How do you like the commune?"

Teresa peered out of the window, noting a large garden off to the side that she'd missed initially. Was that a community garden? Or... "Is this *really* a commune?"

"I don't know, is it?"

She stared at him. "Connor, I feel like I have to ask. Are you...in a cult?"

He laughed. "I don't think so, but can one ever *really* be sure that they're not in a cult?"

"Fair point. I feel like if you have to ask yourself that ques-tion, it's already too late."

"That's a good way to think of it." He buckled his seat belt. "And no – it's not really a commune. Or a cult...I think. This is all temporary-ish housing, mostly for seasonal workers. The busy season on San Juan is in the summer when all of the tourists come to the island. It can be a real problem for people to find an affordable place to stay for a few months, so this really nice guy, Al, opened up his property and built a couple of cabins. He lets people camp here, too, and park their RVs. It's actually pretty fun – I've met some interesting people."

"All of that does sound nice." Teresa put the car into gear. "And subsequently, kind of culty."

"You're right, I should probably revoke Al's access to my bank account."

"Connor!" Teresa laughed. "That's not funny, I can't decide if I need to intervene here."

"You probably should. You seem like something of a cult expert, and I think the leaders would really want to talk to you."

"I wouldn't say that I'm a cult expert. You know, just because I started the San Juan Cult Investigators Society doesn't mean I'm an *expert*. I just consider myself a concerned citizen."

"Uh, maybe the leaders wouldn't want you around, then," he said with a smile. "And now that I'm thinking about it, did you ever notice that cults always seem to start with people who have the best intentions?"

"The Society would love to hear more about your theory, and about what your particular cult's intentions were. Was it to make Christmas decorations fashionable year-round?"

He laughed, shaking his head. "Yeah, I'm not sure what's going on with those."

"Sorry, it was just funny."

"Oh it's definitely funny. There used to be a sleigh with plastic reindeer, too, but the deer have been slowly disappearing, and I'm too afraid to ask what happens to them."

Teresa burst into laughter; she wasn't sure if she was just exhausted and that was making everything so funny, or if Connor was genuinely hilarious. Maybe a little of both.

"But anyway," he said, "it does seem like so many cults attract people who want to make the world a better place. Or who want to improve themselves. It makes it even more... tragic."

She held up a finger. "And that's the lesson – you need to be completely cynical, holding no hopes for a better world, so that no one can take advantage of you."

"Absolutely, words to live by." He nodded, managing to hold a solemn expression for just a moment before laughing again.

As they drove to Friday Harbor, Connor pointed out landmarks and told her the history behind the various buildings and famous islanders. He didn't even seem to realize that he was doing it; he was an effortless tour guide, bursting with excitement. She loved listening to him talk, no matter the topic.

They got into town and Teresa found a parking spot near the restaurant. She was pleased to see that it was rather empty inside when the hostess greeted them at the door.

"Hi, welcome!"

"Hey there," said Connor. "Well, this is kind of awkward, but we have a reservation, under Clifton?"

The hostess nodded and led them back to a table.

Once they were seated, Teresa said, "Looks like we beat the rush."

He laughed. "I swear sometimes it gets so busy in here that you can't get a table for hours. And I didn't want to miss my chance to have dinner with you, I know you don't have time to wait around like that."

She looked down and pretended to be studying the menu. "Well that's – very nice of you to think of it."

She smiled, but she was dying inside. She had a chance to tell him how she felt and instead, she barely managed to string a sentence together. Not her best.

Their waitress stopped by to get their drink orders and asked if they were ready to order food.

"Oh gosh – I'm sorry," said Teresa. "I haven't even looked at the menu."

"That's okay!" She said. "I'll be back in a few minutes?"

Teresa nodded and dedicated herself to actually reading the menu so that she would be ready when the waitress came back.

"I always feel bad when I'm not ready – like I had *one* job and I wasn't able to do it."

"It's not a big deal," said Connor. "But it's nice of you to take it so seriously."

Once their orders were in, Connor asked about her trip to the Seattle airport.

"How did it go? What was the boyfriend like? Was the actress happy to see him?"

"The boyfriend was nice, kind of. He was…strangely giddy to get picked up from the airport. He asked me why I didn't have a sign with his name on it."

Connor shook his head. "You're kidding."

"No, I'm not. But he was mostly joking. I think. And then…I mean, I guess it helped? Our prima donna has been much easier to work with since he's been here."

"Huh. So Chet was right."

She shrugged. "He gets so many ideas that occasionally, yes, he's right."

Their basket of chips and salsa arrived and Connor urged her to try them. She felt like she had no appetite, but she took a bite.

"This is really good!"

He smiled. "If I had a real kitchen, I'd love to cook for you. But right now, I just have a hot plate."

Teresa shook her head. "You're unbelievable."

"What do you mean?"

"I mean that in the best way possible," she said, biting her lip.

"Oh yeah?"

It was now or never.

She cleared her throat. "You're just so...cool. Has anyone ever told you that? That you're just, like *so* cool?"

Connor was drinking his water when he started coughing. Teresa tried to reach across the table to pat him on the back – the best she could do was reach his shoulder.

Once he was able to speak again, he said, "No. Literally no one has ever thought of me as cool. In fact, just you mentioning it almost killed me."

"I didn't want to kill you," she said. "But I do mean it. You're so adventurous and fun and...I've never met anyone like you before."

"You've never met a twenty-five year-old guy with no career, living in a cabin on a questionable cult-like commune?"

She didn't want to laugh at his description of himself, but couldn't help it – he was too cute. And completely unaware of how adorable he looked.

"No," she said firmly. "There's a lot more to you than that cabin. In fact..."

"What?"

She took a breath. "You're way too interesting and fun to be locked up inside a building doing some 'adult job' all day."

Connor smiled and rubbed his eyes. "Well that's kind of you to say, but I don't have a lot of other options."

"Of course you do! The things that you've been doing for the past few years are impressive. And that's coming from someone who would *never* want to do them herself."

"I thought you liked hiking and stuff?" he said, cocking his head to the side.

"Yeah, of course, in my free time. But I'm not going to like – live in a tent. Or spend days backpacking up a mountain. I'd be *miserable* and complain the whole time. Yet you were doing that all day – day in, and day out. And you loved it!"

"Well, yeah."

She continued. "Not everyone is like that. Not everyone can jump into the freezing ocean and keep a smile on their face."

He shrugged. "I guess."

"No, I'm serious. That love you have – that passion? You can't abandon that. And like I said, you're just really cool." She shrugged, and took a sip of water; all of this gabbing was making her dry-mouthed. "It's just that I've been thinking about you a lot, and I wanted you to know that I believe in you, and that...I really like you."

For a while, she wasn't sure where she was going with that sentence. But there it was.

She said it.

He stared at her, eyes searching for a moment before a smile broke across his face. "That's nice to hear, because I really like you too."

She put her hands up. "And I'm not trying to be some sort of motivational speaker here, to get you to build my new commune or anything."

"Good, because you were starting to sound a little – "

She nodded. "I know – culty. You got me thinking about it, and then I felt like I could really run with it."

"That was nice, an inspired start with keeping my personal improvement at the forefront."

She laughed. "Thank you. All right – I won't harp on that any more. How was the screening? I'm dying to know."

"It was…" his voice trailed off, and their waitress reappeared with their food.

They were momentarily distracted. Teresa had ordered the vegetarian options – one roasted cauliflower and one fried tofu poblano taco. She took a bite of each one.

"Any good?" asked Connor.

"They're different – both tasty, but not what I expected. And yours?"

"Really good."

She cleared her throat. "So. Back to the movie screening. Most importantly – did you have to spill soup on anyone?"

He laughed. "No, I didn't. I was as nosy as possible, but it was kind of hard."

"Did you get to see the movie cut at all?"

He shifted in his chair. "Yeah, I did."

"What?" She set the taco down. "What's the matter? What happened."

He looked down then back up at her. "I don't know how to tell you this."

"Tell me what? That the movie was bad?"

He flinched. "Well, you know I'm no movie critic."

"I mean," she let out a sigh. "I didn't think that we were making *Gone with the Wind* here. What did the other people say who saw it?"

"Some of them really liked it," he said, his expression brightening. "They were the people more focused on the nuts and bolts of the zombie genre, I guess. But then there was another group of people...you know, our mob guys?"

"Oh, *they* were there?"

He nodded. "I don't know why, but it sounds like they're investing in this movie. And Chet was asking for more money."

"Oh. Okay."

He seemed to be struggling. "And it didn't sound like they were going to give him what he needed. I feel really bad telling you this, but – "

She shook her head. "You're right – I shouldn't be fishing for information. If I was supposed to know, they would've told me. Please – don't say anything else."

"But – "

"Not a peep!" she said. "Let's talk about something else. Anything else! I don't want to bore you with film talk."

He looked pained. "But I think that you should know – "

She reached across the table and gently placed a finger over his lips. "Not a peep."

He laughed and gently took her hand into his. "Fine. For now."

Teresa felt a jolt in her stomach. She opened her mouth to speak but found it impossible to form a sentence. She squeezed his hand and smiled at him.

"Do you have to go back to work tonight?" he asked.

"Nope. Why?"

"I was thinking that we could stroll through town a bit? I'll be honest – I actually looked up a bunch of history so I could be a better tour guide."

"What else do you have to show me?"

He tapped a finger on the back of her hand. "Well...have you heard of Popeye the seal?"

She laughed. "I don't think so?"

"What! She's *only* the official seal of Friday Harbor! There's even a sculpture of her near the marina."

"Sounds magical."

When they finished dinner, they strolled through Friday Harbor, holding hands as Connor pointed out the different sites and told her about the scandals with the town council and his sisters' efforts to build a new park. It seemed that the things on this sleepy island were more exciting than she ever would have guessed; Teresa joked that it didn't seem *so* far off now that a cult might start here.

She felt like her head was in the clouds – like she was spinning and would never come down.

Teresa caught herself thinking that her life could *literally* not be going any better than it was in this moment.

That was, of course, until it came time for her to drop him back off at his place, and he surprised her with a kiss goodnight.

She drove off in a daze.

Here she was, living her dream and working with a wonderfully talented group of people, when she met the most handsome, sweet, phenomenal guy, completely out of the blue.

Nope – things had never been better.

Chapter 14

This was a problem. Connor had never expected that his snooping would *actually* uncover something important.

He'd managed to enjoy his night on the town with Teresa. It was easy to do – just being around her made him forget his troubles.

But now, in the sober morning light, he had to face the facts.

Or did he?

He spent an hour at home debating with himself and got nowhere. Unfortunately, he was going to miss Sunday dinner because he had to work, so he wouldn't be able to ask his sisters their opinion on the matter.

He sent a text to them to see if they had time to chat about a "sensitive issue." Morgan responded immediately that they were all ears and that he should come over.

When she welcomed him at the door, he immediately second-guessed his decision to involve them.

"Well well well, if it isn't my little brother coming to see the love guru!"

Jade made a face. "I'm sorry, did you just call yourself the love guru?"

"I'm just repeating what we all know to be true," Morgan said with a dramatic sigh. "Otherwise, why would Connor be here? What else could be 'sensitive' enough to warrant our input?"

"Because," he said, cutting in, "if it weren't for you, I wouldn't even be in this situation!"

"What?" She crossed her arms. "What do *I* have to do with it?"

Amanda popped into the living room. "What's going on out here?"

"Connor's finally learning the dangers of getting involved in one of Morgan's schemes," Jade said.

Amanda smiled. "Oh. Did your uncle get back to you already?"

"Uh, Uncle Mike?" Jade narrowed her eyes at him. "Connor, don't tell me that you – "

He let out a sigh. "I might've sent him an email."

"Connor!" Jade stood up from the couch. "You can't do stuff like that! That's serious. What if – "

He shook his head. "He never answered. I'm sure it's fine."

"That's better than what I got from my dad," said Amanda, taking a seat next to Morgan. "I asked him if he could identify the two guys in Teresa's picture."

Morgan snorted. "I can only imagine what he said."

"Yeah," Amanda laughed. "He was like, 'Sure, let me just run this through my facial detection system that we use for all grainy cell phone pictures.' And then he pretended to type on an invisible computer, made a few beeping noises, and told me that he didn't get any results."

"That's actually pretty funny," Connor said, taking a seat.

"Except we still don't know who those guys are," said Amanda.

Morgan leaned forward. "What if I go to the resort pretending to be a rich, exotic heiress? And I try to get those guys to hit on me? And then I can – "

Amanda put up a hand. "You don't have to be an exotic heiress for them to try to flirt with you. They will hit on anything with a pulse."

"Even better!" said Morgan. "And then I'll just, you know, get their names and maybe their social security numbers..."

Jade narrowed her eyes. "Do you remember what happened the last time that you tried to hit on a guy and trick him?"

She shrugged. "As far as I can remember, it went very well."

"It worked, yeah, but I wouldn't say that – "

Connor interrupted the bickering. "Listen, I'm not here to solve the mystery of the weird dudes at the resort. I don't care about that."

"That's right," Morgan said with a nod. "You're here to see the love doctor."

Connor made a face and saw that Jade had made nearly the same exact face.

"I thought you were the love guru?" said Amanda.

"I wouldn't say that I'm here for *that.*" Connor rubbed his face in his hands. Maybe this wasn't a good idea. But who else could he talk to about this? "It's about something that I overheard at the movie screening."

"Oh, were the guys there?" asked Morgan.

"They were – but it's not about that. Not exactly. Chet was asking them for money – more money, because apparently they're involved in this movie. But they said no, and it sounds like Chet is planning on not paying the crew because he's run out of money."

"What!" said Jade. "That's ridiculous!"

Connor filled them in on the exact details of what he'd heard.

"So did you tell Teresa about this?" asked Jade.

He shook his head. "I tried to. I mean – I was about to tell her yesterday when we were at dinner, but we were having such a nice time and she didn't want to hear anything about the screening and – "

Morgan's jaw dropped. "Connor, do you have a *girl-friend*?"

He didn't know how to answer that, so he sat with his mouth open, struggling for words.

"Connor and Teresa sitting in a tree. K-I-S-S-I-N-G! First comes love, then comes – "

"Morgan!" Jade said. "He's not going to tell us anything else if you keep acting like that. This is not how brothers work."

"Yeah!" Connor finally chimed in. "What she said!"

"Why don't you just tell her today?" asked Amanda. "You can tell her the truth – that you didn't want to spoil the evening, but there's something important that she needs to know."

He groaned. "So you think I have to tell her?"

"Yeah," Jade nodded. "I think that it's pretty significant."

"Maybe that's common in the film industry?" Morgan said. "I mean, if she's not getting paid, obviously she knows that. Maybe she's doing it just for the experience."

"Maybe, but I doubt that the rest of the crew wants to work on this terrible movie for free," Connor said.

"Oh, so it's not even a good movie?" asked Jade. "I was thinking maybe they would make the money back in the box office or something."

Connor sighed. "I don't think this movie is going to make it to the box office."

"Oh, that's bad," said Morgan. "You need to tell her. Especially if you like her."

He was quiet for a moment as they all stared at him.

Amanda cleared her throat. "But you're afraid to tell her, aren't you? Because then she has no reason to stay on the island."

He let out a sigh. "Yeah. I know that's crummy of me but..."

"I didn't even think of that!" said Morgan. "Oh my gosh, that's terrible. I've changed my mind, I don't want to be the love guru. This is too hard."

Jade shifted in her seat. "Maybe you could just – "

"No." Connor stood up. "I know what I have to do. Thanks for your help and have fun at dinner tonight. I've got to get to work."

Jade frowned. "Sorry Connor. Let me know if there's anything I can do to help."

He nodded and showed himself out.

Unfortunately, there was nothing that anyone could do to help him at this point. But at least they helped him face the truth.

Connor went home, got ready for his shift, and arrived at the resort a half hour early. He felt uneasy, but decided that he didn't want to go through his entire day like this. There was no use putting it off.

He texted Teresa and asked if she could meet him in the garden.

"Sure! Be there in two minutes."

He knew that it was risky for them to meet at his work, but he couldn't put off telling her any longer.

It was still early, and the garden was completely deserted. Connor took a seat on a bench overlooking the water. He hadn't had much free time to enjoy the island, but it was so engrossing and endlessly beautiful that even little moments like this were stunning.

He sat there, absorbing the calmness of the water as much as he could.

Teresa found him and sat next to him. "Fancy seeing you here," she said with a smile.

"Hey."

Her smile faded. "What's wrong?"

"There's something I have to tell you. I should've told you last night, but we were having such a nice time and – "

"What's wrong? What happened?"

He turned so they were facing each other. "It's about the movie. It's about Chet."

"Oh." She sounded relieved. "I told you, it doesn't matter if – "

"No." He shook his head. "You deserve to know. At the screening, Chet was really desperate to get more money for the movie. And I heard him telling Liv that since he didn't get anything, his plan was to not pay the crew."

Teresa scrunched her eyebrows. "Well, that doesn't mean that...I mean, I'm sure he'll pay us eventually."

"Have you gotten paid at all yet, Teresa?"

She shrugged. "Well no, but there were some issues with the accounts or something. And I'm not in it for the money."

Connor sighed. "I know that you're not, but that's how they get you."

"Cults?" she said, smiling.

He let out a little laugh. "No – these types of jobs. Any time that you're working on something that you really love, and they know that you love it, they know that they can pull this trick. They won't pay you, or they'll pay you next to nothing and say that you're not really dedicated if you're asking about the money."

Teresa sighed. "It's not like that. I mean honestly, I would do this for free."

"You might, but what about the rest of the crew? They probably have families and responsibilities. They need the money. Chet said that he wanted to condense the production schedule, probably so that no one gets wise about it and quits too soon."

Teresa crossed her arms. "I don't understand how this is my fault."

"I'm not saying that it's your fault at all," he said, leaning closer. "It's just a bad situation. And I feel like you deserve to know, and that you probably would want to tell the rest of the crew so that they can – "

"I have spent *weeks* building relationships with these people. I can't burn it all down because you think that the movie is bad and that I'm just some spoiled rich girl who doesn't think enough about money – "

"Whoa, whoa, I never said that! This has nothing to do with – "

"And that I don't know that people have families and responsibilities, and that they need money!"

He cringed. That probably wasn't the best choice of phrase.

Teresa stood. "I have to get going, I'm needed on set."

"I never meant to imply that you – "

"I didn't realize you thought of me that way. I'm sorry for taking up so much of your time."

"Teresa!" He followed her, reaching out to grab her hand. "Please."

She paused for a moment before pulling away. "Have a nice day, Connor."

He stood in the garden, watching as she disappeared into the resort. He hadn't expected her to be happy about what he had to say, but this was a total shock.

Where did that rich girl comment come from? Did he make her feel like he really cared about money or something?

Connor hardly *ever* thought about money – that was his problem. That's why he didn't have any!

He heard a sound behind him and turned around to see Kayleigh standing there. "Midge has been looking for you."

"Oh – I'm sorry. I lost track of the time."

She crossed her arms. "*Clearly* you have no clue what's going on."

Before he could figure out what she meant by that, she turned and walked back into the building.

Connor had no choice but to follow her – and to spend the rest of the day replaying his conversation with Teresa in his head.

Chapter 15

Mike made his way down the trail to the meeting point. He'd been hiking for over an hour and was sure that he wasn't being followed.

That was good – things were starting to heat up, and he couldn't afford to provoke any suspicion. Luckily, no one questioned his long walks. He'd managed to make that part of his undercover persona.

At the meeting point, he found the shovel and dug down three feet until he hit a box. He dusted it off, finding the cell phone inside, as planned.

Promptly at three, the phone rang.

He cleared his throat. "Oregon Coast Rentals."

"Where the sea meets the sea."

He smiled. His boss at the FBI, Lincoln Porter, still insisted on some old school security checks. Mike didn't mind; it was easy enough to remember.

"Mike! It's good to hear your voice."

"It's good to hear yours, too. Did you get my last report?"

"I did. Things are getting touchy."

He sighed. "Yep."

"Listen – we've been monitoring all of your communications. Something strange came in from your nephew."

"My nephew?" Mike paused. "You mean Connor?"

"That's the one. He sent something to your personal email – asking if you recognized two guys from a picture. We've identified them as low ranking soldiers of the Sabini family."

Mike took a swig of water. The hike was rough – he wasn't as young as he used to be. "What business does Sabini have with Connor? Is this your way of telling me that I'm compromised?"

"No, we don't have any evidence to support that."

"Then are they going after my family?"

"I don't think so, I sent some agents into the field to assess and – "

"I need to check this out myself, Lincoln."

He let out a sigh. "I can't let you do that, Mike. Not when you've been undercover for so long. You're the best source we've got, and it seems like – "

"I'm not going to sit over here while a rival family is circling around my little sister."

"She's fine. Ever since her accident she's had her kids over all the time – "

"What accident?"

"We haven't been able to tell you, don't get upset, but – "

"I'm going out. I'll say whatever I need to say to cover my tracks, but I'm going."

There was silence on the line. "And if you blow your cover? Come on Mike, don't be a hothead."

"I've been in for three years, Lincoln. I'm not getting any younger, and we're pretty close to getting agent McKeel accepted."

"But Mike – "

"Three days. I'm leaving in three days, and I'll find a way to explain it."

He didn't wait for a response. He ended the call, tossed the phone back into its box and reburied it.

He'd had enough. Any organized crime activity on San Juan Island should've been reported to him immediately.

Lincoln knew that he didn't have many connections left to the outside world – but he still had some.

And he wasn't going to leave his sister and her kids at the mercy of the Sabini family.

Chapter 16

Physical therapy was difficult for Margie that morning, and she knew that she had no one to blame but herself – she hadn't done her exercises.

Knowing it was her fault didn't help to make it any less annoying, though. She'd been busy all week meeting clients at the barn and setting up for graduation parties. It seemed like she'd have her busiest summer yet, and Margie wanted to be at full strength for it. She promised herself that she would do her exercises for the rest of the week, no matter how busy she got.

Amanda was her ride home, and as usual for Fridays, they made a stop at the coffee shop. Margie always insisted on treating Amanda to something fancy, and this week they both got a new maple tea latte, piled high with whipped cream and drizzled with syrup.

It was, as expected, delicious.

She wished that there was more that she could do to repay Amanda for all of her help over the past few months. Why was Amanda *so* against talking to her physical therapist? Maybe she didn't think he was that cute.

No, that was impossible. He was enthusiastic and adorable, Margie knew it had to be something else. According to Hank, Amanda still wasn't over her ex-boyfriend back in London. That was all that Margie knew about it, though. Hank didn't ask any questions, and Amanda didn't offer any information.

She'd been able to get to know Amanda better over the past few months, but it was slow going. Amanda was a lot like her father, so Margie knew that it would take time for her to open up. She didn't mind; she was just grateful to have Amanda in her life.

She waved goodbye from her front door and then walked straight into the kitchen to get a drink of water. She was standing at the fridge, filling her glass when she heard a voice say, "Hey!"

Margie screamed, dropping the glass as she spun around. It shattered on the floor and she stood, frozen in the moment, before her brain processed what it was seeing.

"Mike?" She reached out a hand to touch him.

"Hey Sis!" He looked down at their feet, then back up at her. "I'm sorry to drop in on you like this – but you never changed the locks."

She stood, mouth hanging open.

He held his hands up. "Don't move. I'm going to clean this up, okay?"

She nodded and kept staring at him. He had no trouble finding the broom and dust pan; they were just where he'd left them, though Margie had updated the cleaning cupboard to her specifications. She watched as he stooped down and swept the glass as best he could.

"Do you still have the old shop vac that I left you?"

"Yes. It's downstairs but Mike – "

He smiled. "Just one more minute, why don't you have a seat?"

She didn't even think to argue with him. She went to the living room and sat down on the couch.

A few minutes later, Margie regained her composure and her brother joined her.

"I didn't mean to scare you," he said, giving her a hug. "I just wanted to make sure that nobody else saw me."

"Is everything okay?"

"Yeah, I think so. I just came back to...check some things out. How have you been? The house looks great – better than it ever looked before."

"Thank you." She cleared her throat. "I've been great! I hadn't heard from you in so long, I didn't get to tell you about Hank – "

"I've been able to get some news," he said with a smile. "Congratulations Mrs. Kowalski."

Margie laughed. "Thank you, but I never changed my name. I'm too old for that nonsense. I wish you could've been there, though – at the wedding."

"Me too, Sis." He sat back and crossed his legs. "You got my gift though, right?"

She paused. "Your gift?"

"Yeah. Remember that ten course dinner that Hank took you to? It was a little late, but – "

"Get out!" She clapped her hands together. "That was you? And Hank didn't even tell me!"

He smiled. "That's because he didn't know. He really thought that he'd won it in a contest. One that he didn't remember entering."

Margie shook her head. "He fell for that hook, line and sinker, didn't he?"

Mike nodded.

"Next he'll be trying to wire money overseas to a long lost relative."

"Yeah, you really should keep an eye on him," Mike said, shaking his head. "The Hank I knew never would've fallen for that. You've probably made him soft."

"Ha. Hank has always been a big softy, you just might not have paid attention."

"Right." Mike smiled, looking around the room. "It's great to see you. And I know that this is a big ask, but you can't tell anyone that I'm here."

Oh. That didn't sound good. "Not even Hank?"

He nodded. "Not even Hank. At least not yet. I might contact him for some official FBI business...though I might be retiring from the FBI soon."

"Really? How soon? When should I plan the retirement party?"

Mike put up a hand. "Please don't plan a retirement party. Ever. And I'm not sure yet. Maybe a few months? Another year? It all depends."

She nodded. "I see."

"No need to worry – I'm not going to try to buy the house back. It's clearly in much better hands with you."

Margie smiled. "It's been such a blessing, Mike. There's so much I want to tell you!"

"Good. Well," he looked at his watch. "I've got about an hour before I need to get going. Are you expecting any company?"

Margie shook her head. "No. It'll be just you and me. I can make some coffee, and I've got some cookies if you'd like?"

He smiled. "Sounds great."

Margie ended up doing most of the talking – both because Mike wasn't really a talker, and because he couldn't tell her much about his own life. She told him all about Morgan, the trial, Jade's divorce, the park, and the accident with the mopeds.

"You don't think that whoever caused that crash did it on purpose, do you?" he asked, his expression quite serious.

"Oh heavens no! It was an accident – an older couple, I see them around now and again. They were driving a moving truck and they just made a mistake."

Mike chuckled. "I bet that Hank keeps a close eye on them now."

"He does tend to hold a grudge," Margie said, smiling to herself. "But no, they absolutely didn't do it on purpose. Is that why you're here? You were worried about the accident?"

He took a sip of coffee. "Something like that. You know, I don't get a lot of information, and when I do, it's a lot at once. I felt like I was overdue for a check in."

Margie nodded and said nothing. She didn't believe him, but it was no use asking questions. Her brother very much took after their father – he was kind, quiet and stoic. Both of them could tell a fib or pull a prank with a completely straight face, and keep secrets to the grave.

It was not a trait that Margie inherited, nor one that she was ever able to develop.

"So what is your plan for retirement, then?" she asked. "Will you be moving back?"

"I haven't really thought about it, to be honest."

"I see. And how long is your visit?"

He set down his now empty coffee mug. "I'm not sure about that either. I might be leaving today, I might not be. But I do have to ask you – if you see me again, if you recognize me – you have to pretend like you don't know me."

"That's very strange. Why can't you tell me what's going on?"

"Because I can't." He shrugged. "And hopefully no one else recognizes me either."

Margie let out a sigh. "All right, Mike. But once you're retired, I will be looking for some explanations."

"You got it." He stood up. "I've got to get going, though."

"Wait – can you tell me one thing? Does this have anything to do with the movie that's being shot on the island?"

He tilted his head to the side. "What movie?"

Margie told him everything that she knew about the production and Mike listened intently.

When she was done, she asked him again. "So are you here because of that?"

"I don't know," he said simply. "Give me a hug and take care. Remember – you can always reach me if there's an emergency."

She squeezed him tight. "There are no emergencies here. Everything is fine!"

"Keep it that way," he said before turning and walking out of the back door.

Margie realized that she had no idea how he'd gotten there; there was no car parked in the driveway and she heard no sounds when he left. It was like he disappeared into the woods!

As lovely as it was to see him, Margie was unconvinced by his calm demeanor. Something serious must've happened for him to come back to the island, and Margie had a bad feeling that she was going to find out more about it – whether she wanted to or not.

Chapter 17

The hits kept on coming. Connor worked the early shift on Wednesday, and just as he was about to leave, Midge told him that the boss was looking for him.

"That sounds ominous," Connor said with a laugh. "Or is Morrow finally giving me that promotion?"

"I'm not sure about that," Midge said.

Connor waited for her to look up and see that he was making a face, but she wouldn't look him in the eye – what was that about?

He walked to Morrow's office and saw that the door was open – he knocked softly to get his attention.

"Hey Connor – come on in. Close the door behind you."

Connor did as he was told and took a seat.

"What's up?" he said.

Morrow let out a sigh. "Listen Connor, I'm just going to get right to it. I have to let you go."

Connor stared at him for a moment. "Okay...can I ask why?"

He fussed with a pile of papers before answering. "I heard about your relationship with one of the guests at the resort."

Shoot. "Listen, it's not – "

"And I was able to ignore it, until another employee came to me with concerns about it. And about you."

Connor leaned forward. "About me? Like, my work? Or about the...guest?"

He shrugged. "It doesn't matter, Connor. You know that gossip spreads like wildfire. And you know the rules. I can't make an exception for you, or it'll come back to haunt me."

Connor let out a sigh. He had a feeling that he knew exactly who started this gossip – not that it mattered.

And not that it wasn't true. There was no denying that he'd broken the rules by spending time with Teresa.

"You'll get paid out through today."

Connor debated arguing his case – he was hardly the first employee to become friends with a guest. And flirting wasn't unusual; even Kayleigh had been unable to resist a dinner invitation from an insistent guest. But perhaps he'd taken it too far by falling in *love* with Teresa...

He stood up. There was no use in arguing. "All right. Well, thanks for everything."

"Take care."

Thankfully, nothing embarrassing happened like being walked out by security. Connor had never been fired from a job in his life though, and he wasn't sure what to do with himself.

He thought about going back to say goodbye to everyone, but decided against it. It was probably best to leave quietly.

On his way out, he caught sight of Kayleigh, watching him through the window. Their eyes met for a moment before she turned and walked away.

There was no doubt in his mind who had gone to Morrow with their "concerns."

Connor considered saying something to her, but what was the point? He'd always treated her with kindness, but missed entirely that she seemed to be jealous of Teresa. There was nothing he could do about that, and nothing he could do about his naive view of the world – as it turned out, not everyone was his friend after all.

He went home and sat in front of the TV for a while, but he couldn't keep his thoughts from drifting. Teresa still wasn't speaking to him – she hadn't answered his calls or any of his text messages. It seemed that the movie was going on as planned, too, so it wasn't like she was in a rush to leave the island.

If only she would talk to him. If only he could explain where he was coming from, and apologize for giving the impression that he thought of her as a spoiled rich girl...

He let out a sigh. He couldn't do any of that if she refused to speak to him.

And now he couldn't even hope to see her at the resort. What was his next step? The restlessness made him pace the room.

Should he look for another job on the island? Or should he actually get serious about applying to "real" jobs?

He'd applied to a handful of places but hadn't been good about checking his email to see if he'd gotten responses. He logged in and it was as expected – nothing from any of the jobs he'd applied to.

He did have an email from his friend Tyler that he'd been too busy to read; Tyler sent out these great, long emails with pictures from his travels and adventures.

They'd met back when they were working as ranch hands. Tyler was a great guy and they'd become close friends. Though Connor knew that he should probably be doing something productive, he felt nostalgic for the days when he didn't have to worry about his coworkers going behind his back.

He opened the email, excited to see what Tyler was up to, and instead was surprised to see that it wasn't the normal format of pictures and funny stories.

No – this was something different. Tyler had only sent the email to Connor and one of their other friends, Jason.

"I've been in Vancouver for the last seven months, and I think that we could start a really great business together. I've been working with a kayaking company that does tours here. We do everything from day trips to weeklong camping trips. I love this company, and the owners are looking to retire. What do you think? We could start our own business! Are you guys in?"

Connor laughed. That was a nice sentiment, but Tyler clearly hadn't thought it out. They couldn't just up and start a business! They'd need money, work visas, insurance, and... kayaks, presumably. How were the three of them going to manage all of that?

Connor closed his laptop. He couldn't take anymore of this today. He changed into his hiking clothes and headed to his favorite spot on the island – Lime Kiln Point State Park.

His first stop was to the rocky overlook where the whale watchers stood and waited for the orcas to swim by. Besides a few onlookers, there was no one else there.

Out on the water, Connor could see a gaggle of kayakers drifting along the shoreline. Their long, orange sea kayaks cut through the water with ease, and the occupants' movements were seemingly effortless.

It looked peaceful, but Connor didn't want to think about kayaks today. Nor did he want to think about zombies, or bad tippers or jobs that required staring at a screen all day.

He followed the trail around Deadman Bay and kept walking into the forest. He hiked rapidly at first, the sound of his steps deadened by the pine needles littering the trail.

After a half hour, he slowed down when it felt like he was finally alone – nothing but the birds, ferns and trees to occupy his thoughts.

He found a small clearing and decided to take a break. After pushing his hiking bag against a rock, he laid back, closing his eyes. He was determined to find peace in this moment, whether or not it felt like his life was falling apart around him.

Connor kept his eyes closed, savoring the crispness in the air and the humming of the bugs overhead. He was slipping in and out of sleep in a pleasantly delirious sort of state where in his mind's eye, he and Teresa were kayaking along the shore, her beautiful red hair glowing in the sun.

Connor heard a voice in the distance, but he tried to focus his attention on Teresa's smile, the glint in her eye, and the way the water moved as she paddled...

"Wake up, buddy."

The image of Teresa faded, replaced with a much harsher voice. Connor opened his eyes and saw that Uncle Mike was standing over him.

He sat up and looked around. Was he really dreaming?

"Uncle Mike?"

"What're you doing out here?" he said, hands on his hips. "Just laying out on a rock for anyone to find?"

"I didn't mean to fall asleep," said Connor, standing up.

Uncle Mike chuckled. "You were always like this – I found you asleep in the yard once when you were a kid. Almost gave your mom a heart attack because she couldn't find you."

"What can I say?" Connor yawned. "It's kind of my thing."

"We should get away from this trail and find somewhere private."

Connor picked a leaf out of his hair. "I didn't know you were coming to visit."

"No one did. And if anyone asks – I was never here."

"Uh – is something going on?"

He smiled. "I'm just following up on your tip. Or did you already forget?"

Connor looked down at his hands and then back up at his uncle. No – this wasn't a dream. The last person on earth that he'd be dreaming about would be Uncle Mike. "No, sorry about that. It was stupid."

"It wasn't. I'm glad that you emailed me."

"Wait, really?"

He cleared his throat. "I know a spot. Follow me."

Connor followed him through the woods; it was a steep climb until the trees around them thinned out and they reached the top of a rocky outlook. The water was a hundred feet below them, and they had a view of Victoria in the distance.

"Do you think anyone followed us here?" asked Uncle Mike.

"I don't think so," Connor said with a shrug. "But then again, I'm not sure how you found me in the first place."

"I'm sorry to tell you, but you're pretty easy to tail."

Connor frowned. "Huh. I guess I should pay attention more."

Uncle Mike shrugged. "I wouldn't worry too much about it."

"So what's going on?"

He took a seat facing the water. "That picture you sent me, do you remember it?"

Connor nodded. "Of course."

"Well, you were right. Those two guys are with the Sabini family."

Connor narrowed his eyes. "Who's that?"

"An organized crime family in New York City."

"Whoa." Connor took a seat next to him. "Really? That's crazy. Wait till I tell Morgan."

Uncle Mike held up a hand. "You can't tell anyone, Connor. Not until I figure out what they're doing here. Okay?"

Connor scratched the back of his neck. "Oh. That's kind of a problem, because everybody already thinks that those guys are with the mafia."

Uncle Mike shrugged. "That's their own fault, then. They stick out like a pair of coyotes in a chicken coop. But you can't confirm anyone's suspicions, okay? It's important to lay low."

Connor nodded.

"I heard that a friend of yours is working on the movie where they hang out?"

"Ah, yeah. That's what got me worried in the first place."

"But they didn't come looking for you, or for your mom?"

Connor shook his head. "No, not at all. I think they're funding the movie. Well, not them – their boss."

Uncle Mike stared at the water before turning back to him. "Interesting. What makes you say that?"

Connor told him about the screening, as well as the issues with the eccentric director.

"This helps, thanks Connor. Hopefully you don't run into them again, and they don't bother your mom."

"Oh...about that."

"What?"

Connor cleared his throat. "They'll be filming a scene at Mom's barn."

"What?" Uncle Mike shook his head. "You have to call it off. That can't happen."

"I don't think that there's anything I can do to stop it."

Uncle Mike frowned. "You can't ask your friend to find a different barn?"

"Not really, it doesn't work that way."

"When is this happening?"

Connor looked down. "I'm not sure, actually. I think on Monday?"

He was quiet for a moment, mulling this over. "Okay. We can make this work. Do you think I could get some pictures while they're there?"

Connor nodded. "Probably. I could take them for you."

"No. I'll be quick, in and out. If you see me, we've never met. Okay?"

Connor nodded.

"Good man. All right, you can get back to napping. Don't tell your mom that we spoke. And don't tell her about those guys – I don't want to scare her."

That was going to be difficult – his mom always seemed to be able to get information out of him. "I'll try, but you know how she is."

He laughed. "I do. It was good seeing you. Sorry about the circumstances."

"It's good seeing you too."

And with that, Connor watched as his uncle disappeared back into the forest.

He sat for a moment, stunned at what had just happened. Maybe it really *was* all a dream?

No – it definitely wasn't. As realistic as his Teresa kayaking dream was, it didn't compare to this.

And now what? Was Teresa in danger working on a set with these guys?

They didn't *look* dangerous. But if it was serious enough for Uncle Mike to show up out of the blue and follow him into the woods, something was definitely up.

Connor let out a sigh. He needed to warn her. He sent another text message; if she didn't answer, he'd have to scour the island until she agreed to talk to him.

Chapter 18

Chet's behavior grew increasingly more erratic. On Monday, he dropped his phone into the ocean while they were shooting, then demanded that Teresa hand over her phone so he could make a call.

He promptly dropped that into the ocean as well.

"My hands are just so cold," he said. "I think I need gloves. Teresa! Please, work on this for me dear. I need you at a hundred percent."

He walked off and she waded into the freezing waters to feel around for her cell phone. It took her a minute, but she found it.

It was completely dead, of course, and not only did Chet not apologize for destroying her phone – he immediately demanded that she go and buy him gloves!

It was too much. She wasn't sure if she could get a new phone on the island or if she had to go to the mainland, but she didn't even have time to look into it. Chet kept her running around like a crazy person for the next few days, and all she had was an old flip phone with dwindling minutes that a fellow crew member loaned to her.

Chet insisted on shooting at two locations simultaneously, with predictable results. They didn't have enough of a crew to keep two separate shoots running at once, and it was a disaster.

In a moment of weakness on Saturday morning, after five nights in a row of getting only four hours of sleep, Teresa cracked when her friend Elena asked if she was okay.

"I don't know," she said. "I think Chet is being extra crazy and things are falling apart."

Elena shrugged. "Don't let him get to you. This is usually when things start falling apart in a production – but we'll pull it together."

"Will we? Chet decided we needed to reshoot three scenes, he broke my phone and I haven't even gotten paid yet."

She frowned. "Really? I thought I was the only one..."

Teresa got a familiar hot feeling all over, the immediate regret for what she'd said. "Oh, maybe it's just a few of us?"

"Maybe."

This wasn't the way to bring this up – not when anyone could overhear. "I don't know – I have to get back to work."

She didn't have time to dwell on her mistake, because Chet had her drive from one side of the island to the other, then to Orcas Island to look for a new location, before ultimately deciding to stay on San Juan Island with the location she'd shown him weeks ago.

On Sunday morning, she hid in her room, hoping to get a moment to herself. She just needed to shower and eat something – then she'd feel better and be able to keep up with Chet's demands.

She'd also hoped that she might see Connor around the resort, but had no such luck. Not that she knew what to say to him – but it wasn't his fault that Chet was a scam artist who probably didn't plan on paying any of them. And it wasn't Connor's fault that she was privileged. And it wasn't his fault that this movie was falling apart, just like he warned her that it would...

No, none of it was his fault. It took her a few days to accept that. When he brought it up to her initially, she felt so caught off guard. She thought...well, she imagined that he meant something other than what he was saying. When he suggested that the rest of the crew might have families and responsibilities, she felt like he was implying that *she* was just there for fun, like it was an eccentric rich-girl hobby.

But when she had more than ten minutes to sit down and really think it over, she realized that he hadn't said anything like what she'd heard at first pass. It was the critical voices in her head that she heard. She heard that she was spoiled, that her dreams were a joke, and that everyone was laughing at her behind her back – the crew, her parents, her old classmates.

That wasn't what Connor said. Not at all. He told her his honest concerns, and she allowed her insecurities to overpower her. And then she lashed out at him, like the fool that she was.

Teresa wanted to talk to him about it, but she hadn't been able to recover her contacts from her old phone, and it seemed like he was never around the resort anymore. Not that she was at the resort much, either. Worst of all, she couldn't get past the bad feeling in the pit of her stomach every time she thought about him and how they'd left things.

Perhaps on Monday she'd be able to see him during the shoot at the barn? That's what got her through Sunday's chaos – the hope that she might be able to mend things with him then.

On Monday morning, however, Chet announced that he had other plans.

"I need you to go to the airport and pick up someone very important."

"What, now?" Teresa shook her head. "But I thought you would need me at the barn – "

"Oh it's fine, they signed the contract, the barn is ours all day, and we even have a permit for once."

Teresa let out a sigh. "I really think that I should be there."

"His flight lands at three. Or maybe five? I don't know – check with Liv. But whatever you do, don't be late."

"Who am I picking up?"

"I am only sending you because I know that I can trust you." Chet lowered his voice. "It's my father."

"Oh! Okay. His name is...?"

"John. But call him Mr. Benzini. Actually, don't talk to him if you can avoid it. Definitely don't talk to him about the movie."

"But don't I – "

"Just bring him to the resort and keep him away from set, okay?"

She nodded. "Okay."

It took some time to track Liv down; Teresa cursed herself for not fixing her phone – she didn't have GPS on the flip phone, and she was awful with directions.

"Check and make sure that the flight is on time," Liv said. "And make sure to leave early in case the ferry is late."

Teresa groaned. "This is all so much harder since Chet dropped my phone into the water."

Liv looked her up and down. "Then get a new one!"

Teresa found a little shop in Friday Harbor where she was able to buy a used cell phone and put her old sim card into it.

It wasn't fancy, but it would do. As she was checking out, her new phone was sounding off with all of the messages and phone calls that she'd missed over the past few days.

There were a few from her mom – whoops! And a few from Connor. The most recent one read, "I'm really sorry and I still need to talk to you – it's important."

She let out a sigh. She didn't know what to say to him, and she didn't have time to think about the perfect way to apologize at the moment.

She was able to pull up the information for the flight – apparently, Mr. Benzini was supposed to arrive in Seattle at 3:45 PM, but his flight was delayed for an hour.

Teresa bit her lip. Technically, she had enough time to pop over to the barn and talk to Connor.

But what was she going to *say*? Except for her one weak moment with Elena, she hadn't talked to the rest of the crew. They weren't *too* far off from finishing filming, so what was she going to tell him? That she was ignoring his warning because all she cared about was herself, and finishing out this movie so she could go on to more projects?

There it was.

She stopped and stood outside of the shop.

That was what she had been unwilling to admit to herself – and subsequently, to Connor as well.

She knew that Connor was right. She was just being selfish, because she didn't want to mess up her chance for a career in filmmaking.

She typed out a message to him, apologizing for being missing in action, and asked if he could meet her at the barn.

When she arrived there ten minutes later, it was chaos – as expected. Half of the crew was back at the warehouse reshooting a scene that Chet decided he didn't like, and the other half was trying to pull off the wedding scene at the barn.

Teresa managed to slip through unnoticed and was hiding behind a porta potty when she gave Connor a call.

"Hey! It's so great to hear from you."

She smiled. "You too. Listen – I'm really sorry, my phone was broken and I only got a new one this morning."

"Oh, what happened?"

"You know – Chet. He borrowed it, then dropped it into the ocean."

Connor laughed. "Of course. Are you coming to the barn today? I was hoping you'd have a few minutes to talk."

"Yeah, I'm here now actually, but I have to get going soon."

"Oh, I'll come and see you. Where are you?"

Teresa cleared her throat. "Well, I'm sort of hiding – behind the toilets. But I'm not sure how much longer I can stand the smell."

He laughed. "I'll be there in a second."

She spotted Connor a few moments later, looking as cute as ever as he walked toward her. She felt panicked – what was she going to say to him? What if he asked about the movie? What if –

"I've got a question for you."

Teresa turned to see that Lenny and his friend had found her hiding spot.

She straightened her shoulders. "What's up?"

"Do you know what Gary Bomba is doing, walking around here?"

Were they playing a prank on her? Teresa looked around – she didn't see anyone unfamiliar. "Gary who?"

"See?" His friend shook his head. "She doesn't even know who he is. You're seeing things."

"I know that I saw him! Are you *sure* that you don't know who Gary is? You never heard Chet mention him? Think real hard."

Teresa shifted her weight. She never thought she'd prefer these guys to be flirting with her; they seemed oddly demanding about this. "I've never heard that name."

"I saw a guy over there," Lenny said, pointing to the catering table. "Older guy, in his sixties. He had on a baseball cap and sunglasses and he was taking pictures. He looks just like a guy I know from – "

His friend cut him off. "You're imagining things, that wasn't him!"

Connor stepped into the circle. "Hey Teresa, can I talk to you for a minute?"

Lenny grinned. "Teresa – what a beautiful name."

She stepped past him. "Excuse me."

"If you see him, tell him that Lenny is looking for him!"

She ignored Lenny and instead followed Connor until they found a place somewhat private.

"What was that about?" asked Connor.

"They were looking for some guy named Gary?" Teresa shrugged. "Lenny said he saw someone. I have no idea. But I really don't like talking to those guys."

Connor's eyes widened. "Yeah, you should avoid them at all costs."

Teresa took a step back. "Wait, what? Why?"

"It's – complicated. But who were they asking you about?"

"Who knows," she said with a sigh. "Some older guy? They said he was taking pictures."

"Oh. They saw him where?"

"By catering, I guess." She looked at her watch. "Shoot. I have to get going soon, to get Mr. Benzini from the airport."

Connor laughed. "Who is that? A new lead actor?"

"I wish. It's Chet's dad."

Connor tilted his head. "Benzini? I thought Chet was French."

Teresa laughed. "I know. I have *literally* no idea what's going on right now. It's been total chaos, I haven't been able to sleep because Chet has me just running around at all hours, and he broke my phone so I wasn't able to talk to you all week and say that..."

Something was caught in her throat. It was so dry – had she had any water today? That was another area of self-care that had fallen apart in the last few days.

She cleared her throat and spoke again. "I wanted to say that I'm sorry about last week. I'm sorry about what I said and..."

She trailed off and Connor jumped in. "No, I'm sorry about everything. I don't know what I was talking about, clearly – "

She held up a hand. "No, you were right. I just couldn't – "

"What are you still doing here!" Liv yelled from the barn. "You needed to leave, like, yesterday!"

"On my way!" Teresa yelled, forcing a smile.

She turned back to Connor. "I'm sorry, I have to get going. But maybe we can talk later? Are you working tonight?"

"Ah...actually, I don't work at the resort anymore."

"Oh?"

"They weren't happy about us spending time together."

Teresa felt her stomach drop. "Are you serious? Connor, I'm *so* sorry, I can't believe that you lost your job because of me."

He shrugged. "It's fine. Maybe we can talk later when you have some time?"

"Sure." Her phone went off – it was Liv. The woman had no tact!

Teresa groaned. "I'm sorry – I really have to get going. But I'll text you?"

Connor nodded. "Sure – I'll be around. Any time."

She smiled at him before rushing off. She managed to get her car in line for the ferry to Anacortes; as she was sitting in her car waiting, she replayed her conversation with Connor and burst into tears.

She'd been *so* mean to him! And he lost his job because of her! How had she allowed everything to fall apart so spectacularly?

Chapter 19

Poor Teresa. She'd looked positively worn out. Her braid was loose, with bits of hair flying around her face, whipped by the wind. She had bags under her eyes and Connor was pretty sure there was a coffee stain down the front of her shirt.

Chet must have *really* pushed up the production schedule. But at least now he understood why Teresa hadn't responded to him – at least she didn't hate him. That was the best news he'd had all week.

Once her car disappeared down the driveway, Connor turned his attention to looking for Lenny.

Was the "Gary" that Lenny thought he saw actually Uncle Mike? That seemed impossible – Uncle Mike was too smart to be spotted by those two idiots.

But then again, Lenny was sure that he saw something and was on a mission to find the mystery man.

Connor decided to follow Lenny around from a distance, pretending to be interested in the various comings and goings on set. He could see the increased pressure on the crew – things were much more harried now, and people were obviously stressed out.

Chet was nowhere to be seen, but there were a lot of frowning faces and shouting that he hadn't ever witnessed before.

Connor made two full trips around the barn and didn't see anyone resembling his uncle. Perhaps he'd gotten the pictures that he needed and left? Or maybe he was better at blending in than Connor realized.

He was about to go back and hang around the catering table when he nearly stumbled into Lenny and his friend.

"I'm telling you, I know what I saw."

The friend shrugged. "Yeah, so what?"

"So what?" Lenny squared off with him. "*So what?* If Dmitry sent one of his guys out here, how do we know that Benzini didn't decide to work with him instead?"

"Oh come on, after we sunk a million dollars into this kid's movie? Get outta here."

Lenny shook his head. "I don't know, man. What is this place anyway? Is this like a bed and breakfast? Gary could be staying there."

Oh boy. That was not good. They were *not* forgetting about this Gary character, and now they were zeroing in on his mom's house!

"What're you looking at?" said Lenny, glaring at Connor.

He cleared his throat. "Sorry, just trying to figure out if we need more pastries."

Lenny made a face. "Pastries? Aren't you that kid from the resort?"

So much for going undetected. "Yeah, I work with...catering."

He nodded slowly. "Is this part of the resort? That little house there?"

"Oh, no," Connor shook his head. "That's a private home. Nothing to do with the resort. We're just renting out this barn for the day, for the shoot."

The friend looked him up and down and whispered something to Lenny.

He decided that it was time for him to get out of there. He smiled before turning and walking off.

Connor didn't want them to see him going into the house, so he took the long way down by the water and made sure that no one was watching him before he slipped into the back door.

Shoot. *Now* what was he supposed to do? He needed to talk to Uncle Mike – but how?

He didn't have a phone number for him – not one that worked. He could try emailing him again, but that might take too long...and he needed him to know about the connection between Benzini and the mob guys as soon as possible.

Connor pulled out his phone and googled Chet Benzini. Unlike Chet Laret, there were actually a few interesting results. None of them had to do with filmmaking, of course.

Connor could see why Chet thought it was a good idea to change his name. The second result was a mug shot from an arrest for petty theft from a Coach store.

He shook his head – what did Chet steal from a Coach store? A fancy backpack? A fancy purse?

He tried to search for Chet's father, but he had no luck. All he had was a last name – Benzini. Uncle Mike would probably have no problem finding the guy, all of his known associates, where he lived, heck – even where he liked to have breakfast.

So how was he going to find Uncle Mike?

The front door opened and his mom and Amanda walked in.

"Connor!" His mom called out. "It's nice to see you here."

"Hey Mom. Hey Amanda."

Amanda waved. "I have to run to the restroom – I'll be right back."

His mom set her bag down. "Is everything okay honey? You look very distressed."

"Oh, it's nothing."

She frowned. "You know that you should never lie to your mother."

"I'm not."

She kept staring at him.

He knew that she wasn't going to let him go until she had something. He sighed. "I got fired. From the resort."

She gasped. "What happened?"

"It's nothing, I got in trouble for fraternizing with a guest."

"Oh," she nodded knowingly. "Teresa."

"It's fine, I'm not worried about it. And they're out there filming in the barn right now. Actually – I need to go and do something, maybe Amanda can stay here with you? And, uh, lock the doors?"

"Lock the doors?" She tilted her head. "Why would we need to barricade ourselves inside, Connor? I thought I might go and sneak a peek at this exciting movie."

"No, definitely don't do that," he said, much too quickly.

She eyed him. "Do you not want me embarrassing you in front of Teresa?"

Connor cleared his throat. "What? No. I just need to get going. Hey, by chance have you heard from Uncle Mike?"

Her eyes widened. "Who? Me? No. Uncle Mike? Why?"

"Well..." Connor paused. His mom had always been a terrible liar. "Have you talked to him recently?"

"No," she shook her head. "I have not. I wouldn't say *recently*."

They both stared at each other for a moment. Connor was about to ask her another question when Amanda walked in.

"What's up guys?"

AMELIA ADDLER

"Oh, hey," said Connor. "Can you stay here with my mom for a bit?"

"I do *not* need supervision!" she called out from behind them.

His stare with Amanda was unbroken. "Please?"

"Sure, no problem."

"Thanks."

He gave his mom a kiss on the cheek and had his hand on the front door when he turned around. "Can you lock this door after me?"

Amanda nodded. "Sure."

It made him feel better that his mom wouldn't be alone there, though hopefully it wouldn't take him long to find Uncle Mike. The island wasn't *that* big. He got to his car and pulled out his phone.

Connor wasn't sure how to get his uncle's attention – did he need to go hiking in the woods again? Fall asleep on a kayak in the middle of Haro Strait?

He wasn't sure. But whatever he needed to do, he was going to figure it out. There was no time to waste.

Chapter 20

"What's gotten into him?" asked Amanda as she locked the door behind Connor.

"I'm sure I have no idea," Margie said, hands on her hips. "You know, I've got to go and send some emails. For the business."

Amanda nodded. "Sure. I think I'll just work on my laptop in the living room if that's okay?"

"Fine by me!" said Margie, rushing off.

Amanda stood there for a moment, trying to piece together everything she'd heard. When she was in the bathroom, she couldn't help but overhear Margie and Connor's odd conversation.

Now Connor took off in a hurry, and Margie was acting strangely – though admittedly, walking impressively fast. All the physical therapy was doing wonders.

Something was up. She wasn't sure what, exactly, but *something* was going on.

Amanda settled into the couch but couldn't focus on her work. She sent a text to Morgan, asking her if she knew why Margie and Connor were acting so odd.

Morgan wrote back right away. "I don't know, could it be because the mafia is shooting a movie thirty feet away?"

Amanda laughed. Morgan would not give this up.

She wrote a message back, "Normally, I wouldn't agree with you, but Connor told us that we need to stay away from the filming and lock the doors."

"Really?"

"Yeah. I don't want to get caught up in the hysteria, but... I'm just saying, things are very strange here."

"Do you know where Margie keeps her pepper spray?"

Amanda laughed. She really needed to catch up on work stuff and *not* get caught up in mob mania – she had a project due and couldn't spend the day playing cops and robbers.

But then again...this was more interesting, even if it was all made up.

Despite feeling crazy doing it, she got up and went to the closet where her dad kept a spare taser. Amanda was good with tasers. Her dad insisted that she learn how to protect herself, and she'd spent many hours practicing, yelling out commands and deploying the taser at dummies.

Amanda felt the weight of the taser in her hands. It had been some time since her dad made her practice, but it felt familiar. What was the harm in having it next to her as she worked?

She went back to the couch and started opening up emails that she'd missed from her boss when she was driving Margie back from physical therapy. She was in the middle of reading a particularly confusing chain when she heard something.

Amanda froze.

Or at least, she *thought* she heard something. She sat still, listening.

There was nothing, except for the sound of Margie typing away in the other room.

Amanda rolled her eyes. She shouldn't be getting caught up in this stuff. She opened the most recent email from her boss that, for some inexplicable reason, was written entirely in caps.

"THIS WAS SUPPOSED TO BE ON MY DESK LAST WEEK!"

She cringed. What was she talking about? Amanda was pretty sure that it wasn't even her client, but she needed to double check that she hadn't promised anything...

There was a thump downstairs.

She stopped.

That *was* a real noise.

She quietly closed her laptop and picked up the taser in her left hand. Her dad had tried to teach her to use it with her right hand, but she was a lefty. It was more comfortable that way.

She slipped her cell phone into her back pocket and quietly crept toward the stairs, standing out of sight and listening.

Now she could hear it all more clearly; there was *definitely* someone down there, bumping around, opening and closing drawers.

Amanda pulled out her phone and dialed 911. But before she got a chance to talk to the operator, she heard the footsteps getting closer to her.

Yikes.

Amanda stepped so that her legs were shoulder-width apart and held the taser in front of her. She shifted the safety off as her dad's words repeated in her head.

Aim at the lower torso.

Aim at the lower torso.

Aim at the lower torso, *square and steady.*

A man appeared in her line of sight at the bottom of the stairs.

"Whoa whoa whoa," he said. "What are you – "

"Stay back!" Amanda yelled. "I have a taser!"

He put his hands up. "Come on sweetie, why don't you and I have a talk?"

He took a step toward her, holding his arms up, and Amanda caught a glimpse of a holster beneath his unzipped tracksuit jacket.

"Get out of here!"

"This is all a misunderstanding," he said with a smile, slowly walking toward her.

"Get out! Do not come any closer!"

He stepped quickly now, clearing three stairs at once, rapidly closing the distance between them.

Amanda gritted her teeth. Square and steady.

She pulled the trigger of the taser, launching the probes directly at him. One landed on his abdomen, the other on his leg. It was almost as if he was suspended in midair for a moment before he dropped to the ground.

Amanda was a little surprised that it worked. She stood, stunned, before again hearing her dad's voice in her head. *Secure the area.*

She rushed over and told him not to move. His gun was now fully exposed, sitting in the holster.

She pulled it out and stared at it, checking that the safety was on. Who *was* this dude? Why did he have a *gun?* And why did he break into the house!

Margie appeared next to her. "Amanda, *what* is going on?"

"Here, take this!"

Margie shrieked. "I can't take that!"

The man was groaning and starting to sit up. He looked vaguely familiar, but Amanda couldn't quite place him.

"Do not move or I will turn this back on," Amanda said firmly.

He obeyed, flattening out on the ground. "Listen lady, you got this all wrong. I'm just looking for my friend Gary."

Amanda looked at Margie, then back at him. "Gary? Gary who?"

He kept his hands raised above his head. "I thought he lived here, it's a misunderstanding, there's no need for this."

"You broke into the house and then came running at me."

"That's *your* opinion and – "

"Do not move until the cops get here."

He started to speak again when Amanda heard her dad's voice booming through the house.

Wow, the 911 operator must've been on the ball!

Within an instant, he found them, and Amanda felt her muscles starting to relax.

Another deputy handcuffed the guy and Amanda was able to hand off the gun as well.

"I want nothing more to do with that," she said, letting out a little laugh.

Her dad grabbed her by the shoulders. "Are you okay? Amanda? Margie?"

"I'm fine!" said Margie. "I had no idea that anything was even happening until I heard Amanda screaming at this guy!"

"What happened?" He wrapped her in a hug. "I'm so glad that you're okay."

She tried to shrug but he was squeezing too tightly. "That guy broke into the house. I heard him messing around downstairs, so I called 911, and then when he came after me, I tased him. Just like you taught me."

He laughed. "That's my girl."

"Thank goodness you were here," said Margie. "But I am going to *kill* Mike."

Amanda and her dad both turned to look at her.

"What's this?"

She smiled. "Uh...Hank honey? I think we need to talk."

Chapter 21

His first idea was to go back to Lime Kiln where his uncle had found him last time. Connor rushed up the trail and realized that he didn't remember exactly where they'd cut through the woods.

After almost forty minutes of wandering around, he decided that maybe there would be some clue that his uncle left for him in his cabin.

He drove back home and after looking through everything, Connor was disappointed to find that there was nothing but his usual mess.

He sat on his bed and tried to think. It seemed like his mom was acting funny when he mentioned Uncle Mike. He hadn't stopped to think about it at the time, but the more he did, the more it seemed like she was hiding something...

Connor pulled out his phone to call her and realized that it was dead; he *really* needed to get better about remembering to charge it if he was going to live in normal society, and not out in the woods. He plugged it in and let it charge for a few minutes before trying again.

He had a missed call from Teresa, and a voicemail.

"Hey Connor, it's me. I mean – it's Teresa. I just wanted to call and check what's going on. I got a frantic call from Liv that there were a bunch of police cars at your mom's house, and the noise was ruining their shoot. I don't care about the shoot, obviously, but I just wanted to make sure that everything's okay? Give me a call back when you get this – I'm just sitting in traffic."

Connor felt sick. Police cars at his mom's house? He never should've left her there!

He dialed his mom's number, stomach churning with every ring.

"Hello?"

She answered!

"Mom! Are you okay?"

"Yes I'm fine – everything's fine."

"Teresa said that there were a bunch of police cars around the house? What's going on?"

"Well…" There was silence for a moment. "We had a little commotion here…but everything's fine. We can talk later."

Connor frowned. "What kind of commotion?"

"Oh, it's nothing. I'm glad that Amanda was here, she – you know, I'll tell you later. I'm talking to Deputy Iams and making a statement."

"Oh, sorry. I'm glad to hear you're okay!"

"Of course. Love you!"

Had Chet done something crazy at the house? Or maybe his mom called the cops because some zombies ended up at her back door? It didn't sound like she was upset, but she was still being evasive…

Connor had had enough guessing – he got back into his car and drove to his mom's house. When he got there, there were two police cars out front and he spotted Matthew leaning over his car and writing on a notepad.

"Hey!" he called out as he approached.

Matthew waved. "Hey Connor, how's it going?"

"Not bad, I guess. I heard that something happened?"

Matthew nodded. "It did. Hank asked me to hang back while he questioned the guy at the station."

"What guy?"

"The guy who broke into your mom's house."

Connor stopped. "*What?*"

Matthew tucked the notepad into his pocket. "Oh, sorry, I thought you knew? Some guy from the movie set snuck into your mom's house."

"But she's okay?"

Matthew nodded. "Yep. Amanda tased him. Chief was so proud – says that she gets her aim from him."

Connor stood for a moment, trying to absorb this information. "That's crazy."

"You're telling me. You know how stupid you have to be to break into a cop's house?" Matthew said with a laugh. "Not just a cop – but Chief?"

Connor rubbed the back of his neck. "Yeah, pretty stupid. Is it okay if I go inside?"

"Of course."

There was another deputy talking to his mom inside. She waved when she saw him and he waved back, but instead of interrupting them he decided to talk to Amanda.

"I heard that you saved the day."

She laughed. "Yeah, I guess so."

"What happened?"

"I don't really know, honestly. I was hoping that you could tell me. Before you left, you and Margie seemed...on edge?"

Connor took a seat next to her. "Yeah..."

"Did you know that guy? Connor, is this the," she lowered her voice, "*mob* dude that Morgan got me paranoid about?"

"Well..." He shifted in his seat. Uncle Mike told him that he shouldn't talk to people about this, but now Amanda was involved. It wasn't possible to be more involved than tasering someone. "It's complicated."

"Complicated like I'm going to have the mob coming after me?" Amanda asked.

"I mean...I don't think so? And I hear that you have really good aim so – "

Amanda sighed. "He said he was looking for someone named Gary? Do you know who Gary is?"

Aha. So it *was* Lenny. Probably. "Maybe we should find somewhere quiet to talk?"

Amanda nodded. They went downstairs, out of earshot of the deputies and Margie.

"Start talking," said Amanda. "If I have to flee the island, I would at least like to know why."

"Okay, I don't think it's *that* dramatic," he said. "But I suspect that 'Gary' is my Uncle Mike."

She cocked her head to the side. "What do you mean?"

"You *really* can't tell anyone this. Do you swear to me?"

"I swear."

He sighed. "So you know how I told you that my uncle works for the FBI?"

"Yeah, you weren't supposed to tell me that either, right?"

"Right. And the reason that we don't talk about it is because I'm pretty sure he does some undercover work."

Her eyes widened. "Are you serious?"

"Yeah. So when I sent him that picture, apparently it started a whole cascade of problems. Because those two guys actually *are* from a mob family."

Amanda gasped. "Oh my gosh. You're kidding, right? You are not telling me that I just tasered a mob guy."

"I mean, I don't think he's the head of the family or anything. My uncle just wanted to figure out why they were here. He was worried it had something to do with him."

"And does it?"

Connor shook his head. "I don't know, but I don't think so. I'm trying to find a way to contact him and tell him what other stuff I found out but...he's like a ghost. There's no trace of him."

"Well, he seemed to think that 'Gary' might be in the house."

Connor laughed. "He's not. And I'm really sorry, I was on set and heard that Lenny – the guy I'm guessing broke in – was looking for some guy that he recognized. I panicked, and I wanted to find Uncle Mike and tell him but...well, then this happened."

"Oh, *that's* where I knew him from. I saw him on set that day. I just couldn't think when it was all happening."

"Ah, right."

"Okay, great." Amanda stood up. "I'm going to pack my bags. Does my dad know about this yet?"

"I'm not sure. And don't freak out yet. We need to talk to my mom. I get a feeling that she knows more than she's letting on."

They went back upstairs and waited until the last deputy left the house.

Connor gave his mom a hug first. "Amanda told me what happened. I'm glad that you're okay."

"Yes! Just fine. Thanks to her."

Connor turned toward Amanda. "Yeah – what you did was amazing."

Amanda smiled. "I'm glad I was here. Though I *do* wonder who that guy was."

"Just a loon, I guess!" his mom replied, turning to walk into the kitchen.

Connor and Amanda shot each other a look before following her.

"Mom," Connor said slowly. "Did Uncle Mike mention where he was staying?"

"Not to me, no," she said.

Connor cracked a smile and his mom spun around.

"Connor Clifton!" she said, pointing at him. "You should not trick your mother like that!"

He put his hands up. "I just asked you a question, which you then chose to answer."

She threw a dish towel onto the counter. "Connor, you can't be getting involved with these things. It's dangerous!"

"Well, now we're all kind of involved," said Amanda.

Connor spoke again. "I talked to Uncle Mike yesterday. He had some questions about the movie, and now I have more information to tell him. So I do actually want to know where he's staying."

"Well, I honestly don't know," she said, letting out a sigh. "I'm just hoping that Hank gets home soon so we can hear more about this intruder."

Amanda nodded. "Me too. I'd like to know if I need to go into hiding."

"You are not going to have to go into hiding!" She turned back to the fridge. "Are you kids hungry? I have a lentil soup in the fridge. And some fresh bread that I got at the bakery this morning."

"That sounds great, actually," said Connor. He hadn't eaten all day. "I'm just going to give Teresa a quick call and let her know that everything is somewhat fine."

Connor stepped into a bedroom and shut the door before calling Teresa.

"Hi!"

"Hey, how's it going?"

She let out a sigh. "Oh you know, just inching along the highway. How are you? Is everything okay?"

"Yeah, I think everything's fine. One of the creeps from set tried to get into my mom's house."

Teresa gasped. "Are you serious? Why?"

"I'm not sure yet. But he was tased by Amanda. So that's pretty funny."

"That is insane!"

"I know. I don't want to distract you while you're driving, but I just wanted to give you the update. Things should be quiet for them again."

"That's good. I can't believe that I'm saying this, but I'm glad I'm not on set right now. I think it's been total chaos."

"I think it was chaos before you left. So don't feel bad."

"Oh – it looks like Liv is calling me. Talk later?"

"Sure."

It was nice just to hear her voice. Connor stood, smiling to himself for a moment, before rejoining his mom in the dining room. They didn't have to wait long for Chief to come back; within the hour, he walked through the front door.

"Oh good, you're all here," he said, taking a seat.

Connor's mom got the most important question out of the way first. "Are you hungry dear?"

He shook his head. "I'm okay, thanks honey."

"I'll just get you a little bowl of soup," she said, walking to the kitchen.

"Thanks for hanging around guys, I can take it from here."

"They know everything," his mom yelled from the kitchen.

Connor and Amanda smiled.

Chief let out a sigh. "Great. All right – well, listen kids. You can't tell anyone about this stuff. Not yet. This includes Morgan and Jade, do you understand?"

They both nodded. Connor felt like he was sitting in the principal's office.

He continued. "The good news is that it seems like Lenny is convinced he made a mistake in breaking into the Chief Deputy Sheriff's house."

"So I won't have to go into witness protection?" asked Amanda. "I know that he's in the mob, Dad."

Chief rubbed his face in his hands. "Yes, he's a soldier – not terribly high up, but not harmless either. He's not exactly known for his intelligence, and it seems like he's most worried about keeping this dumb move of his quiet."

"Good," said Amanda.

"Have you heard from my uncle?" asked Connor. "I need to tell him some things."

Chief nodded. "He'll be here soon, once the movie crew clears out."

"You knew he was here too," Connor's mom interjected, "and you didn't tell me!"

Chief smiled up at her. "You know that the FBI likes to work with the local sheriff. In this case, it just happened to be me."

She let out a huff and shook her head. "Mike could've saved us a lot of trouble by telling us who he was talking to."

"That wouldn't have been as mysterious," said Connor.

"And you wouldn't have felt as special," added Amanda. "I seem to be the *only* person he left out."

"And yet, you did the best of all!" Chief said, winking at her.

She laughed and rolled her eyes. "Right."

The wait was agonizing for Connor, but as promised, an hour after the last crew member left the barn, Uncle Mike appeared at the back door.

"Hello!" he said after stepping inside.

"Do you know that you're impossible to find?" Connor said, unsure if he felt more relieved or exasperated.

He smiled. "I get that a lot."

Connor's mom walked up and poked Mike in the chest. "You almost got us *killed*!"

"I'm sorry!" he said. "I'm really sorry. I only came out here in the first place to make sure that they hadn't connected you to me."

"And now...they know?" asked Amanda.

Chief cut in. "No. It's just Lenny, and he knows that he screwed up big time breaking into my house."

"That's great news," Uncle Mike said. "I'm going to leave the island tonight. I don't want to cause you guys any more trouble."

"Wait! I found out more stuff. I don't know how Lenny changed his tune now, but he definitely *thought* that he saw you on set – when you were taking pictures."

Mike frowned. "Well, that's not good."

"And he was worried that you were going to end up working with someone named Benzini? Do you know who that is?"

He was quiet for a moment. "I don't think so."

Connor smiled. So he *was* useful after all. "Apparently, it's Chet's father. My friend Teresa had to go and pick him up from the airport today – they're probably coming back by now. But I heard Lenny saying that they put a million dollars into this movie so that they could work with Benzini, and they were worried that *you* were going to take that business away from them. You and someone named Dmitry?"

"Wow," Amanda said, turning to look at him. "Nice work Connor."

Chief nodded. "Yeah, not bad."

His mom was just staring at him. "Were you going to tell me *any* of this?"

"I was! Just...after I told Uncle Mike."

His uncle stood up. "That's really interesting stuff, Connor. You got more information than I managed to get. And I'm glad that they don't know we're related, but now I have to figure out what brought them here. I'll be in touch."

"That's it?" His mom said. "We haven't seen or heard from you in three years and you're just going to disappear?"

He laughed. "Margie, I promise that when I retire you'll end up being sick of me. But until then, I have to go for a bit longer."

She let out a sigh and gave him a hug. "Fine. But how about next time before you almost get me killed, you give me some warning?"

"Deal."

He agreed to take a few sandwiches for the road, and then disappeared once again.

They settled onto the couch, planning to watch a movie to soothe their fried nerves.

Connor knew that he should be more worried about the newly confirmed mafia connection to San Juan, but all he could think about was Teresa.

Was she in danger? Would Lenny leave her alone? What was Chet *thinking* working with these people!

He knew the answer to that, at least – Chet didn't care. All he cared about was "redefining the zombie genre," and starring in his own awful creation.

But Connor wasn't sure at all about what he'd tell Teresa when they spoke. He couldn't tell her about the mob exactly... but he couldn't very well leave her totally in the dark.

At least they were talking again. He was hopeful that tomorrow he might get a chance to actually patch things up.

Chapter 22

It was easy for Teresa to follow Chet's instructions about not speaking to Mr. Benzini. From the moment that he got into her car at the airport, until the moment that she dropped him off, he only spoke to her twice.

The first was when he initially got into the car.

"There's been a change of plans," he said. "You won't need to drive me to Anacortes."

"I'm happy to do it. I – "

He cut her off. "I'll be going by seaplane. I'm not one for sitting in traffic."

Teresa smiled. "Of course."

"I just need you to take me to the Lake Union seaplane terminal, please."

"No problem."

Teresa plugged it into her GPS and started driving. It was a much shorter trip than driving all the way back to Anacortes and taking the ferry to San Juan Island.

Chet had probably planned the longer trip on purpose so that his dad wouldn't be able to see anything, but it was a weak attempt at keeping him away. Mr. Benzini did *not* seem like a man who could be kept away from anything.

She couldn't wait to tell Connor about it. He didn't look like a mafia guy – not at all. He was older, probably close to her dad's age, and dressed impeccably in a well-fitted suit. He had salt-and-pepper hair, neatly trimmed, and similar features to Chet. He was kind of a silver fox!

If Teresa didn't know any better, she would think that he was some sort of a movie mogul. But as far as she knew, Chet didn't have any experience or real connections to the movie industry.

Mr. Benzini spent the rest of their short trip working on his laptop in the back of the car. When she dropped him off, he politely thanked her and handed her a hundred dollar bill.

Teresa was flabbergasted when he put it in her hand, but before she could try to give it back to him, he disappeared.

"Crap!" She said, stuffing the bill into her pocket. She had to get ahold of Liv or somebody – anybody – to warn them that Mr. Benzini would arrive on the island much earlier than planned.

Liv didn't answer her first call, but she did answer her second.

"This had better be an emergency," she said.

"It is. Chet's dad booked himself a seaplane – he's on his way now."

Silence. "You were right. This is bad. Thanks for the call, I'll handle it."

The call disconnected. Teresa was relieved – it seemed that Liv knew that there was no point in yelling at her. What could she possibly have done to stop a man as intimidating as Mr. Benzini from doing what he wanted?

And now there was nothing left to do but drive back and catch the ferry.

Teresa got stuck in traffic on the way back, as expected. By the time that she got onto the ferry and parked her car, she was exhausted. Her lack of sleep was catching up to her, and this was the first time that she was able to shut her brain off in a long while.

She got a coffee and settled into a comfortable seat near a window. It was hard to believe that it was just this morning that she'd left the island – it felt like it was weeks ago. Maybe it felt that way because she'd been dying to talk to Connor again...to sort her thoughts and tell him the whole truth. He hadn't texted her back yet, though, so she had to wait.

The ferry hummed along and between the beautiful view of the water and the quiet in the cabin, Teresa felt herself relaxing. She was almost lulled to sleep when her phone went off.

She slowly reached into her purse to pull it out. It was a text message from Elena. "Hey Señorita, are you back from Seattle yet? A bunch of us are getting tacos tonight at that place in town. Are you in?"

"On the ferry right now! I can meet you there in about half an hour."

Well that was a good sign! If the crew wasn't working late into the night, maybe things actually went well that day – once the police had cleared out and everything.

Teresa got off of the ferry and drove straight to the restaurant. It was the same one where she'd had that lovely dinner with Connor. Maybe if shooting was going better now, she could have a little more control over her schedule and find some time to talk to him.

She needed to explain why she reacted the way she did. Not that there was any excuse for how she behaved, but she at least needed him to understand where she was coming from.

Teresa walked into the restaurant and was surprised to see that it was almost entirely full with members of the crew. She saw Elena and waved hello before making her way over.

"Wow! This is quite an event."

Elena patted her on the shoulder. "Welcome to your first wrap party."

Teresa narrowed her eyes. "What? I thought you don't have a wrap party until you're done shooting."

She sighed. "Well, half of the crew walked out today. And the other half is just having a party before they leave tomorrow. So...I think we're done shooting."

"What?" It felt like the room suddenly decided to spin. "Is this a prank?"

"Sadly, no. I talked to a couple of people who said they also haven't been paid. Which is, you know, not a *huge* deal. A lot of people never end up getting paid for their work on a movie. But it turns out that Chet stiffed the wrong people."

"What do you mean?"

"I mean that there are people who you *can* get away with not paying, and then...everybody else. He hadn't paid any of the cameramen, or the makeup artists that he flew in from LA. I mean, I think they got paid after the first week, but nothing since. And with no zombie effects or cameramen...it's going to be hard to finish the movie."

Teresa took a deep breath. "Oh. I see."

"Don't look so glum! We'll find another one. I got a friend who said he's getting a lot of work up in Vancouver. I'm thinking I'll head up there next. He works in post-production – I could ask if he's got something for you? I know you're into that."

Teresa looked up at her. "I am! Yeah – that would be incredible."

"I'm not sure which software he uses to edit...I think it's Avid. Do you know how to use that?"

"Yeah. And I know Resolve, too."

"Awesome. And don't worry! This happens sometimes, and I'd say it's no loss to the world if this movie is never seen. Get yourself a margarita and relax."

Teresa nodded. The noise around her made her feel increasingly far away. Since she didn't know what else to do, she decided to take Elena's advice and walked up to the bar to place an order.

She'd just taken her first sip when the bartender handed her credit card back.

"Sorry – I tried your card three times and it's not working."

Teresa frowned. "Oh I'm sorry – I'm not sure what the problem is. Here – I have another one."

She watched as the bartender swiped the second card. After a moment she turned to her and shook her head. "Sorry – not this one either."

"Uh...I don't know if something happened with my bank, but I have some cash."

Luckily, she had that tip from Mr. Benzini in her pocket. Her trip to get the silver fox proved useful after all.

After paying, she stepped off to the side and pulled out her phone, planning to log into her bank app when she saw that she had a message from her mom.

"Call me. Now."

She groaned. She knew that it would come back to bite her that she was hard to reach for so long. Normally, her mom wanted a call every day as well as a text to let her know she was going to bed. She'd done her best, but she was brief on the phone since things were so busy and she had limited minutes on that borrowed phone.

Teresa went outside and gave her mom a call.

"Thank goodness you're okay!" her mom said immediately.

"Hey Mom – I'm sorry! My phone was broken for a few days, remember? I called you from my friend's phone? And I texted you today as soon as it was fixed, but I had to drive down to Seattle to get – "

"Well you should've called," she said. "I'm guessing I finally got your attention with the credit cards."

"Oh. That was you?"

"You left me no choice. I need to talk to you."

"Sorry Mom, things have just been really busy with the movie and I've been working a lot."

"Honey, your dad and I have been thinking, and it's time to put an end to this. When is the movie done? We want you to come home. You've had enough."

"Actually...it's going to be done really soon. But I have a lead on another job and I was planning to – "

"The deal was one movie, Teresa! You've had your fun. You should be studying for the LSAT, not running around chasing some wild fantasy."

"The deal was for one *year*," said Teresa. "And it's only been – "

"Well, I've changed my mind. And your father agrees. I'll unfreeze your card when you agree to come home."

"But Mom!"

"No 'buts' Teresa! I'm worried sick about you. And do you know how hard it is to have to explain to everyone what you're doing?"

"Why does anyone care what I'm doing?"

"Because you have a promising career ahead of you. The way you're acting, though, makes people wonder."

"Let them wonder! Mom, I don't care what people say, I want – "

"Life isn't about what you *want*, Teresa. It's not a fairy tale. Life is about what you *need* to do. I'm not having this fight with you again. I called the resort and told them that you'll be checking out tomorrow. That's final. Good night."

Teresa pulled the phone away from her face and dropped it into her purse. She stood against the wall, feeling like the wind had been knocked out of her.

Just like that, it was over? All because she hadn't kept in touch as much as she was supposed to, and that made her mom nervous?

Or maybe it was because the people at the country club were talking. Who knew?

It didn't matter. The end result was the same – her mom made the decision that enough was enough.

Never in her life had Teresa gone against her mom's decisions. Teresa had always been the golden child – the baby who could do no wrong. She did well in school, never broke the rules or snuck around, and her parents always gushed about what a perfect kid she was.

Teresa understood from a young age that she was lucky to be so privileged, and that she needed to take advantage and not squander opportunities. Her parents had always been so proud of her, but now...

Now they were just embarrassed.

And who was Teresa kidding? She knew they were right. She knew that she was an embarrassment – this dream, this fantasy that she was trying to live out. What was more pathetic than a rich kid trying to "make it" in Hollywood? How was she any better than Chet?

The door opened and Elena popped her head outside.

"Hey, I was looking for you!"

Teresa waved her over. "Oh, I'm sorry, I had to make a call."

"Is everything okay?"

Teresa forced a smile. "Yeah, everything's fine."

"Come on, don't get upset! Movies fall apart – directors get in over their heads. It happens. Everyone here knows how great you are to work with. It'll make a difference in finding you more work – I promise. I texted my friend in Vancouver and he said that he'd be happy to take you on. Plus, when I told him you're Canadian, he said that makes it ten times easier. No work permits!"

Teresa sighed. "That's so nice of you Elena, I really appreciate you reaching out to your friend. But...I think I have to go home."

Chapter 23

After all of the excitement passed, Connor decided to stay over at his mom's house for the night. She was delighted, of course, and insisted on making an elaborate breakfast the next morning before he drove her to physical therapy.

After that, she wanted to be dropped off in Friday Harbor to meet with her book club and have lunch.

Connor was happy to oblige, and the reality of what had happened the day before was finally hitting him. As happy as he was that he could help Uncle Mike put some things together, he knew that he would *never* want a job in law enforcement or the FBI.

He just didn't have the stomach for it. The thought of Lenny getting into the house and threatening his mom made him feel physically ill.

The question was, though, what *did* he have the stomach for?

He hadn't had much time to think about it, but Tyler's idea of starting a business didn't seem like it was right for him, either. He still wrote back to Tyler, asking some questions about the plan; he didn't want to leave his friend hanging.

It just didn't seem possible for them to start their own company. Jason was on board, and Tyler appeared to have thought about a lot of things, but it seemed too good to be true – another fantasy. And Connor needed to keep his head in the real world.

There was still no word from Teresa. Knowing how busy she was, he didn't want to stress her out by asking again when they could talk. He figured if he hung back, she'd let him know when she had some free time.

After dropping his mom off, Connor decided to head back to the house and check out whatever Chief was up to. He'd taken the day off to install a new security system, saying that he'd been thinking about installing one for some time, but never got around to it. And now, of course, he regretted waiting.

"What's the verdict, Chief?" Connor asked as he hopped out of his car.

Chief stood in front of the house, a concentrated look on his face. "I'm not sure yet. But I'm trying to decide where to put the cameras, and how many we'll need. I think we'll need at least two for the full length of the house..."

"Well, if you need anybody to climb up on the roof, I'm your man."

"What?" Chief looked him up and down. "Do you think I'm too old to get up there myself?"

Connor shook his head. "No, nothing like that. Although..."

"What?"

"If we're looking at a ratio of risky activities to injuries, you have a much worse record than I do."

He laughed. "Don't you have somewhere that you need to be? Someone else to harass?"

"Not really," Connor said with a shrug. "I don't know if Mom told you, but I got fired."

Chief pulled out a measuring tape and motioned for Connor to grab the end. "Oh yeah – your mom mentioned it. You got canned because of your girlfriend, right?"

"She's not my girlfriend, exactly."

"Why not?" Hank frowned, scribbling the measurement he'd just taken onto a scrap of paper.

"We kind of...hit a snag."

"Oh. That'll happen." Chief nodded.

"I'm waiting for her to call me."

"I see." Chief stared at him for a moment, arms crossed over his chest. "So what's next Connor? Are you waiting for the FBI to call too? And offer you a job?"

"Absolutely not. Uncle Mike seems to know everything that's going on around him at all times, while I can barely see what's directly in front of me," he said with a laugh. "I'm not really sure what to do. There's a lab in Seattle that I might apply to."

"I never got the feeling that you wanted to work in a lab."

"I don't, really. But I also don't want to be thirty years old and still living out of a tent."

Chief shrugged. "You like tents."

"Yeah, but that's not a long term solution. It's not a career."

"You can find a way to make it one. You're a smart guy. You'll figure it out. What you really don't want to do is be thirty years old, or forty years old, or heck – sixty years old and be trapped in a life that you never wanted."

Connor looked down at his shoes. He wasn't used to talking to Chief this long without making fun of each other. "Yeah. I don't know. A friend of mine had an idea to start a business."

"Oh yeah? What kind of business?"

"Sea kayaking tours – in Vancouver. They've got their own resident orca pods – did you know that?"

"Sure."

"But I don't know, it doesn't seem like a good idea."

"You don't like sea kayaking?"

Connor shook his head. "No, it's not that. I think it'd be awesome. But it's just like – another dream. How long are we going to make it work? Will it be another two seasons and I'll be looking for a new job?"

"What's the chance of you never forgiving yourself if you don't at least try?"

He sighed. "I don't know."

"I don't know either, kid." Chief handed him the tape measure again. "But I can tell you one thing – you're really dragging your feet on this new job. I've been hearing about you applying to this lab in Seattle for months. And in my experience, that's probably because you don't *really* want to do it."

"But I know that I *need* to do it. It's just that after I met Teresa, she made it seem like..."

"Like what?"

Connor shrugged. "Like...anything was possible. I mean, she's working on this insane movie and not letting anything stop her. Not even the fact that her family thinks she's nuts and the director actually *is* nuts."

"She sounds like a smart girl. What if you – " Chief's phone rang. "Hang on a sec – let me see who this is."

Connor nodded and as soon as Chief answered the call, he could hear his mom's voice blaring through the speaker.

"Everything's fine honey. Connor's right here, helping me get some measurements." Chief shot Connor a look. "Okay I'll tell him. Connor – your mom said that she tried to call your phone and it went straight to voicemail, so she panicked."

"Oh shoot," Connor pulled his phone out of his pocket – it was dead.

Again.

He hadn't even thought of looking for a charger in his mom's house the night before; his phone was so old that usually no one had a charger that worked for it. And all morning he'd been waiting to hear from Teresa!

"Sorry – no battery. I'm going to go inside and charge it."

Connor went into the house and found a charger that fit his phone – he felt rather silly when he realized his mom already had left it out for him, plugged in next to the bed. She thought of everything.

He left it for a few minutes and went to make some tea. When he got back, he saw that he had a missed call and a voicemail from Teresa. He wanted to kick himself.

It started, "Hey Connor, it's Teresa."

He frowned. Her voice sounded so small.

There was a pause before she spoke again. "I hate to do this, but I tried to get ahold of you and haven't been able to. Uh...the movie fell apart. So I guess it's kind of good, since you won't have to worry about anyone else harassing your mom. But ah, I talked to my parents and they told me that I have to come home. I'm getting ready to leave the island right now. Maybe we can catch up later? I'll be driving home for a while... I'm really sorry about how we ended things. And – I'm sorry that I'm rambling. I'm just sorry about everything. Goodbye Connor."

He listened to the message a second time; he couldn't believe what he was hearing. How had the movie fallen apart?

And why were Teresa's parents telling her that she had to go back home?

And why was she listening to them!

He was sitting in the kitchen, feeling dazed, when Chief walked in.

"What happened? You look like you got hit by a bus."

"I *feel* like I got hit by a bus," said Connor. "I missed a call from Teresa – she's leaving."

"Leaving the movie?"

"Leaving San Juan Island. The movie is done, apparently. She said it fell apart. And now her parents are making her go back home. She's probably on the ferry right now."

Chief frowned. "What do you mean her parents are 'making' her?"

"It's a long story. Her parents are – well, they want her to be a lawyer and go to work for the family law firm. They told her that she could try filmmaking, but if it didn't work out, she had to come back."

"That's a good one," Chief said with a chuckle. "Could you imagine me trying to tell Amanda what to do?"

Connor smiled. "Yeah, but Amanda is different."

"Do you think that I wouldn't like to tell Amanda that she has to live on this little island with me forever? Of course I would." Chief shook his head. "But it would never work. And I'd never want to make her unhappy."

"Are you saying that Teresa's parents *want* her to be unhappy?"

"No. I'm sure that they're doing what they think is best. They just happen to be wrong."

"Yeah," Connor said with a sigh. "Very wrong."

"Well?"

"Well what?"

Chief slapped him on the shoulder. "What're you going to do?"

Connor shrugged. "About what?"

"About everything!" said Chief.

Connor jumped a little – he wasn't used to Chief being so energetic. "I don't know."

"Come on Connor. You can't just let things keep happening to you. Sometimes, you've got to decide what you want, and then you have to go after it."

"That's the thing. I've never been good at that."

"Well now is a great time to change, then."

Connor fidgeted with his phone before tossing it onto the counter. "What am I supposed to do, Chief? Am I supposed to call up Teresa's parents and tell them that she's not going anywhere?"

Chief made a face. "I'm not sure that you have to involve them, but sure. Then what?"

"I don't know. I feel like I don't know anything!" He looked down at his hands. Maybe Kayleigh had been right all along and this *was* just like *Dirty Dancing;* Teresa's wealthy parents were going to whisk her away forever.

"I'm not buying that, Connor. You know things. What're you going to *do*?"

"Sure Chief, I guess I could go and rent a boat, chase down the ferry, and tell her that she's too incredible to waste away doing what she's told."

Chief nodded. "Okay, now you're getting somewhere."

"Except I don't have a boating license, so instead all I can get is a kayak...but that would be *way* too slow, and I would never catch up to the ferry."

Chief's eyes brightened. "I've got a boat."

"Yeah," Connor said with a laugh. "Right."

"I do. And we've got the Marine Patrol boats, too. If you wanted a little bit of pizzazz, I could put the lights on."

Connor stared at him before finally saying, "I can't tell if you're kidding or not."

He smiled. "Is Teresa a chase-down-in-a-sheriff-boat kind of girl?"

"Yeah." Connor felt a chill run down his back. "She is. That I know for sure."

"Okay then." Chief pulled his keys from his pocket. "I can work with that."

Chapter 24

Was it colder on the ferry today, or was Teresa imagining it? Maybe she was just cold because she'd been up most of the night, trying to figure out what to do.

She'd called her dad to plead with him, to let her have the full year like they'd agreed on, but he wouldn't budge. Before he ended the call he said, "One day, I promise you'll thank us for this."

In this moment, it was hard to imagine how that could be true. But at the same time, she was so profoundly embarrassed by her failure and how she'd behaved that she was inclined to believe him.

When she'd called Connor that morning, it was a relief to get his voicemail. Teresa was too embarrassed to face him – too ashamed to admit that he'd been right about everything. And it was just harder to face the truth when she felt so low.

It was her own fault that things have fallen apart so spectacularly. Not with the movie, exactly. But maybe if she had been honest with herself and honest with the rest of the crew, they could have figured something out. Maybe people wouldn't have gotten to their breaking point and disbanded the movie entirely.

Teresa felt bad for everyone, even Chet. Sure, he was kind of delusional and sometimes difficult to work with, but he had a vision. And he'd always been kind to Teresa, in his own way.

When he insisted on keeping her nearby to shield her from Lenny, it made her feel special. It made her feel like there might actually be a place for her in the crazy world of filmmaking.

If only that were true.

Now she understood – everything had shifted into focus. If she'd been honest with herself about how desperate she was to make this movie work, maybe she'd have noticed things falling apart sooner. Maybe she could've admitted to herself that this might not be the *smartest* horse to hitch her wagon to. She could've avoided saying those awful things to Connor.

It was too much. Her parents were right – this was silly. All of it was silly, but especially her. Teresa knew now that she only had herself to blame.

They were getting close to Anacortes, and she decided to go to the back of the ferry and watch the islands disappear. Maybe one day she'd be able to visit San Juan again – when she had her own money and her own career.

Maybe after working as an attorney for a few years, she could save up enough to take a sabbatical and try filmmaking again. It would take a while, but at least she might have more sense then and some control over her own life. Maybe she wouldn't behave in such a desperate way.

It was windy out on the deck, but there were a few people standing around, chatting and admiring the view.

The sky was gray and filled with clouds, matching her mood. She leaned against the railing, looking down at the water churning beneath them. It was a beautiful scene, but alas, it was not for her. It was a dream, a place that she would be able to return to whenever she closed her eyes, but not somewhere she could stay.

Teresa was staring off into the water when the passengers around her began talking excitedly.

"Look how fast they're going!" said a little boy standing a few feet ahead of Teresa, pointing ahead.

She followed his finger to see that he was pointing at what looked like a police boat – its lights flashing as the hull slammed through the waves.

Soon, everyone on the deck was watching and there was a murmur of voices. It looked like the boat was coming right for them.

Teresa wondered if Morgan had been right all along and the San Juan County sheriffs were looking for fugitives on the ferry.

Or maybe just Lenny.

She didn't have to wait long to find her answer. The boat pulled up alongside of the ferry and a voice boomed out from it.

"This is the San Juan County Chief Deputy Sheriff Hank Kowalski with a message for Teresa Timmons."

Teresa looked around – was she hallucinating?

"Attention Teresa Timmons!"

This was a different voice. It sounded almost like... Connor?

"By order of the San Juan Cult Investigators Society, you are requested to remain at the Anacortes ferry terminal for an important initiation. I repeat, your presence is needed at the Anacortes ferry terminal."

Teresa laughed.

This was the first time that the San Juan Cult Investigators Society was mentioned, long after she made it up on that first date with Connor. But it seemed to have grown into a rather powerful institution if it had the sheriff on its side now.

She stuck her hand into the air and waved at the boat. Some people around her started to clap and it felt like her cheeks would crack from laughter.

An announcement went over the ferry speakers that they would soon be docking and that drivers needed to return to their cars.

Teresa did as instructed, but as soon as she was inside her car, she pulled out her phone and saw that she had a message from Connor.

"I am so sorry that I missed you earlier," it read. "I forgot to charge my phone. Again. I couldn't let you leave without saying goodbye."

She wrote back. "Message received, loud and clear. I'll see you at the ferry landing?"

He wrote back immediately. "Perfect."

She never realized how long it took to unload a ferry, but when she was finally off, she was able to pull her car off to the side.

Connor was standing nearby, the boat docked behind him.

"How do you like my ride?" he asked with a wide smile.

"Very pretty," she said. "And surprisingly fast. Is it yours?"

He laughed, shaking his head. "No. My stepdad offered to give me a ride after I realized that you'd left."

"Oh."

Connor turned around and waved. "Thanks Chief!"

Chief responded with two loud honks, and then started the engine.

"Do you have time to go for a walk?" asked Connor.

She was in no hurry to get home. "Sure."

"There's a great trail just a few miles away. Do you mind driving?"

"Not at all."

She followed his directions until they found themselves in the parking lot for a little park. There were people playing volleyball on the beach and grilling; it was quite peaceful.

"There's something I'd like you to see," he said.

Teresa smiled. She was happy to go along with whatever he had planned – especially because it would likely be the last time she ever got to be swept up by his beautiful smile. "Okay."

They started along a trail and Connor asked her what had happened with the movie. She explained the issues with the crew getting paid and ultimately, with people quitting.

"So, you were right," she said. "I should've told everyone a long time ago that Chet had run out of money and wouldn't be paying us."

"No, it's hard to know what was right," he said. "I mean, I just overheard something. It's not like we knew for sure."

Teresa shook her head. "No. I was there, I saw what was going on. I just didn't *want* to see it. I didn't want to see that Chet was desperate, and that things were falling apart. And it's because..."

He turned to look at her. "What?"

"It's because I was desperate, too. I needed this movie to work. So I couldn't admit to myself that the acting was bad, and that Chet was unreliable and unprofessional. And I couldn't admit to myself that you were right, because that meant I'd have to give up on my dream. I know that sounds stupid – "

"That's not stupid. Not at all."

She let out a sigh. "It's my fault. I know that now. I refused to see what was going on in front of me, and then it all came crashing down."

"I don't think you can hold yourself responsible for Chet being a disaster."

Teresa laughed. "Still, it doesn't matter. My parents are done waiting around for me to play filmmaker. My mom called and checked me out of my room. She wants me to come back and apply to law schools."

"Is that what you want to do?"

"No, what I want is for Chet to pay the crew, so we could finish this movie and I could go on to another one."

"Okay..." He smiled at her. "But since that's not in your control, what do you really want? Do you want to go back and do what your parents tell you to do? Or did you like working on the movie?"

"Like it?" She looked down, kicking a rock out of the path. "I *loved* it. It was amazing. Even when things were kind of terrible, it was still great. I felt like I was really part of something. For the first time in my life, things felt...right."

"Okay then. There's your answer."

She laughed. "My answer to what?"

"You can't go back. You can't go back and study for the LSAT, you have to keep doing what you love."

"I can't just do that, Connor! My parents – my mom – she's not like your mom. She's...intense."

Connor laughed. "Oh please, *my* mom is intense. Do you know that she pepper sprayed the guy who burned down my sister's house?"

"Wait, really?"

Connor nodded. "Oh yeah. Don't be fooled by her sweet demeanor, she's a fighter."

"My mom's a fighter too," said Teresa. "She was the first person in her entire family to go to college, and she started the law firm with my dad. They've built an empire. And if I don't go and take my place in it, she's going to cut me off totally. She already froze all of my credit cards. And this is embarrassing, but I don't have much of my own money."

"I see. That's the best she can do?"

Teresa spun to face him. "What do you mean 'the best she can do?' We never fight, and we hardly ever argue. This is the worst disagreement we've ever had – she – "

"I just mean – the best she can do is take away the resort? A place you never even wanted to stay?"

Teresa shook her head. "It's more than that. It's not really about money. By going against her, that means I'm…"

"What?"

"A disappointment. A failure. And I don't want to disappoint my family. They mean everything to me."

Connor stood for a moment, then looked out over the water. "I can understand that."

"So…I have to go back."

She pressed on, following the trail into the forest and up a winding path.

Connor followed behind her for a while, silent. Before too long, they reached the top of a hill.

"Come here – there's something you need to see," Connor said, cutting over to a side trail.

He offered his hand to help her clear a particularly rocky part of the path. She had the urge to hold onto his hand forever – but that was silly. She let go as soon as she reached the top of the rocks.

What she saw took her breath away – it was a two hundred and seventy degree view of the water. They were standing at the top of a cliff, and near the edge hung a single wooden swing from an old madrona tree.

"Go ahead," he said with a smile. "Take a seat."

She looked at him and shook her head. "No way! That looks terrifying. What if I fall off?"

He gently took her hand again. "It just looks scary. Look – you can't actually fall off of the cliff. I mean – you'd have to go flying like twenty feet out."

She couldn't take him looking at her with those big blue eyes. She sat on the swing and gripped firmly to the ropes on either side.

Connor got behind her and gave her a gentle push. "See? It's not so bad."

"I guess you're right – it's a long way to the edge. But it feels like..."

He gave her a more swift push and she shrieked.

"It feels like you could die at any moment?" he said with a laugh.

She put her foot down to stop the swing. "Yes. It's kind of mesmerizing in a way – it's so beautiful here, but completely terrifying to be on this."

"You don't have to sit there if you don't like it."

She turned around, studying him. "No. I like it."

Teresa started swinging again and he offered a few gentle pushes.

"You know," he said, "you really changed how I think about everything."

"I have?"

"Yeah. When I came back to the island, I'd kind of given up. I planned to help my mom, work a little bit at the resort, and finally grow up."

"I know, you were going to totally give up on your dreams."

"Kind of like you are now."

She sighed. "That's different. I already tried to follow my dreams, and I failed. It's...embarrassing. It's worse than embarrassing."

"You didn't fail! You're doing amazing. You're probably doing so well and are so involved that it scared your parents. They realized that you were never going to come back and do what they wanted."

She sighed. "Maybe."

"You're really inspiring, do you know that? If it weren't for you, I would've thought that there was no other way."

"Real inspiring," she said. "Especially when I made you lose your job."

"I didn't even like that job. And now, because of you, I'm going to take a chance."

She turned around. "Really? What kind of chance?"

"Starting a sea kayaking tour company. In Vancouver."

"Vancouver, huh?" Everything seemed to be happening there all of a sudden...

"Listen, I know that this is a lot to think about all at once but...I believe in you, Teresa. I think that you're unbelievably driven, and smart, and on top of all of that, you're *so* pretty."

She hid her face in her hands and let out a laugh.

"No, I'm serious," he said. "Like, *distractingly* beautiful. And if you want to go back and go to law school, I think you should. But if you want to go somewhere else, *anywhere* else, and chase down your next job – I know that you can do it. I know that you'll make it because you're amazing. And no matter where you go..."

She turned around. "What?"

"No matter where you go, I know that I'll never be able to stop thinking about you. And this is a lot, I'm just so...I just need to say this. But we could do a long distance thing. And I can come to visit? I just can't – I can't bear to watch you drive away and out of my life forever."

She stood up. "I thought you'd think I was an idiot after working on this stupid movie, and your mom's house being broken into, and – "

He took her by the hands. "No. I've never thought that about you. You take risks, so yeah, sometimes you get it wrong. Big deal."

She laughed. "I just...I actually might have a job in Vancouver."

His eyes widened. "Are you serious? What kind of job?"

"My friend Elena – she said she could get me an editing job."

"That's great!"

"But Connor – I don't have *any* money. I mean, my parents pay for everything. It's pathetic. Even if I wanted to rebel against them, and I'm not sure that I do, how would I go about doing that?"

"You're talking to the right guy here," he said. "I mean, I *literally* lived in a tent for a month. Not to say that you have to live in a tent, too."

She laughed. "Okay."

"But Teresa – come on! That's the least of your problems. Your parents had to convince you that you needed their support, because otherwise they'd have no power over you. I'm sure we can find a place for you to live – granted, with a lot of roommates – but you can make it work. I promise. I'll help you, I've started over in new places without any money a hundred times."

She looked away, her eyes lingering on the water crashing into the jagged rocks. The ocean didn't have to ask anyone for permission to rise and fall...

He continued. "Trust me. I know that you can do this. I can feel it in my soul."

He took her hand and placed it on his chest.

For whatever reason, she believed him. "Okay."

"Okay?" He leaned down so that their foreheads were almost touching.

"Okay. I'll try it your way." She leaned in a little closer. "Do you know where I can get a cheap tent?"

He smiled. "I know a guy."

He gently touched her chin, pulling her closer and kissing her.

Teresa didn't know how this was going to work, but in that moment, she wasn't worried at all.

Chapter 25

It wasn't hard to find Teresa a place to stay on San Juan. Connor first called Amanda to see if she knew of any old friends who were renting on the island, or of any hidden gems in general.

Amanda was happy to help, though at first she assumed he was sick of living in the cabin. After he gave her a brief synopsis of Teresa's situation, Amanda volunteered to let Teresa stay in their house for free for as long as she needed. Connor thought it was a decent enough idea.

"I don't want to be a bother," Teresa protested.

Connor shook his head. "You won't be a bother – not at all. Amanda said that as long as you don't mind sleeping on an air mattress, you can stay there as long as you like."

"I don't mind that at all!" Teresa said, eyes bright.

Connor loved seeing that joy in her again. "Believe me – my sisters are *thrilled* that they can keep you in their house and interrogate you. Consider yourself warned."

"I'll be fine."

"No really – they will talk your ear off."

"You forget that I have two brothers," Teresa said, "and actually having someone who *wants* to talk sounds great."

Connor shook his head. "Be careful what you wish for."

"All of my wishes are coming true," she said as she kissed him on the cheek. "And they're better than I imagined."

He smiled. "Mine too."

The rest of the day flew by. Connor took Teresa over to the girls' house to get her set up. While Jade and Amanda helped get her settled, he checked his email and saw that Tyler had answered his email.

It was long and full of detailed explanations. Most of his concerns were addressed, and Tyler had clearly thought things through. There were no sure things in life or business, of course, but Tyler was serious and sincere in this effort.

Connor found the idea of it overwhelming, but Chief was right – he couldn't just wait around hoping that the right thing would happen to him. He had to make those decisions for himself, even if there was a risk of failure.

Especially if there was a risk of failure.

If Teresa could do the same thing under the harsh scrutiny of her parents, what excuse did Connor have?

Once things were set up, they left the house and went into Friday Harbor to celebrate. Connor took Teresa to the brewery – his treat – and they sat outside on the patio, absorbing the glorious blue sky and the last moments of warm sun on their faces.

Teresa was different now – seemingly lighter, though she still had concerns.

"When am I going to call my parents and break the bad news that I'm not coming back?" she asked, taking a sip of her cider.

"Whenever you feel ready. I can pretend to be them and we can practice if you'd like?"

She laughed. "No, that's okay. I know what they're going to say, more or less. What's hard is that…"

Connor waited for her to continue, but she seemed to be struggling. "What? That they're going to be upset?"

"No, not exactly – though they will be. What I dread most is disappointing them. I know they're going to be *so* disappointed."

Connor let out a sigh. "Yeah. It seems like there's no avoiding that."

Her face fell. "Yeah."

"You're not the only one, you know."

"Sometimes it feels like I am. Especially with my brothers being so successful."

"Nah!" Connor shook his head. "Every year, *millions* of kids disappoint their parents by going into the arts."

Teresa laughed, hiding her face in her hands. "That's true."

"And even though my parents weren't like that, I have a lot of friends whose parents were disappointed that they weren't doing something different. You know, the usual stuff – they wanted them to become doctors, or lawyers. I guess most people aren't proud that their kid is working on a ranch, no matter how beautiful it is."

"You know that you're pretty lucky in that regard."

Connor smiled. He was exceptionally lucky, in more than one way. "Yeah. But you're not the only one. This is, I think, an age-old compromise. And it's not like you have some crazy expectations that you're going to be a famous director and redefine the zombie genre, or something."

Teresa burst out laughing. "Yeah, on the scale of delusions, I'm really not that high. I just want to make an honest living. I don't want to be famous, and I don't think that I'll be redefining anything."

Connor nodded. "Yeah. You love the work itself. I think that's a good sign that you're headed in the right direction."

"Well, I don't think that I can call them today," she said. "My head is still spinning. I honestly can't believe that I'm doing this."

"Take your time. Maybe make sure that you've got that job in Vancouver first?"

"Yes, that's a good idea. And I can write out a six month plan, so I don't have to go into the conversation blind."

"Sounds smart to me."

She let out a breath, relaxing her shoulders. "So what do you want to do tomorrow?"

"Well, I know a lot of good hikes. Or we could rent some kayaks? And I can get a feel for what I'll be getting into."

"Oh that sounds cool!" said Teresa. "I'm game for anything."

"There's just one thing..."

"What?"

"Tomorrow my mom is having her usual Sunday dinner. And I'd like for you to come, but I have to warn you that my family – well, they can be a lot."

"Jade and Amanda were perfectly nice today! And I would love to finally be able to go to Sunday dinner."

He couldn't very well *not* invite her, but for some reason, the image of Sunday dinner made Connor more anxious than starting a business or moving to Vancouver.

Maybe it was his concern that Uncle Mike might show up and need to talk about more mafia business? Connor couldn't tell Teresa the details – in fact, he didn't even want to *know* the details. If he could, he'd leave the island tomorrow and never have to deal with another suspicious individual again.

But no, that wasn't it. Uncle Mike would be smart enough to wait until everyone left, or invent some cover story if he did need to crash the dinner.

Connor didn't know exactly what concerned him most – Luke's commentary, Morgan asking a hundred questions, his mom or Chief saying something...

Really, it was the risk of Teresa being scared away in general. Connor had never felt this way about anyone before, and his instinct was to hide her away.

He tried to push it out of his mind by enjoying the kayaking tour that they took in the morning. Teresa wasn't the most coordinated kayaker, but Connor didn't mind – he steered their kayak and was happy to do most of the paddling.

It was so much like that daydream he'd had that day in the park – except it was better, because it was real. They didn't get to see any orcas, but they did see a handful of porpoises and stellar sea lions. Teresa seemed to glow in the sunshine, and he tried not to stare too much when they shared a quiet, peaceful lunch on the beach.

The kayaking trip went too quickly, and before he knew it, it was time for dinner. He briefly considered faking an illness to get out of it, but knew that it wouldn't work.

It was now or never – for everything, it seemed.

Chapter 26

When they got to Mrs. Clifton's house, Teresa was immediately swept away by Morgan and given a tour. Dinner was served shortly after, so Teresa didn't have much of a chance to ask questions.

During dinner, Teresa was relieved that most of the attention wasn't focused on her. Instead, the full force of the teasing fell on Chief Hank for his unique use of a sheriff's department boat.

"We were all surprised when we heard that you wanted to take a turn on Marine Patrol," said Matthew. "At first, we thought that maybe Krispy Kreme was having a sale on the mainland."

Morgan laughed. "I just assumed that it was normal for Chief to take a boat out, park in the middle of the ocean, and take a nap."

"Very funny," Chief said, narrowing his eyes. "I'll have you know that I'm a skilled sailor and that's why I don't have to practice often."

Matthew held up his hands in an apparent surrender. "I'm just relaying what the rest of the deputies told me, Chief. It brings me no pleasure to speculate about Krispy Kreme."

Connor looked at her and smiled. He was being oddly quiet. She smiled back and squeezed his hand under the table.

"I think it was romantic," said Jade with a smile. "Not just of Connor, but of Chief too."

"Very romantic for the two of them, indeed," said Luke. "I wish I'd been there to film it. Perhaps we can do a reenactment? You know, show the softer side of the sheriff's department?"

Everyone laughed and Chief shook his head. "I'm not in it for the fame, Luke. I'm in it for the donuts."

Teresa decided to speak up. "Do you make a lot of movies, Luke? Outside of your work?"

Luke shook his head. "Sadly, not so much anymore. I used to. But then..."

"He got lazy," Morgan said.

Luke pretended to look hurt. "I resent that! Things have been...busy. I have a demanding work partner."

Morgan nodded. "That's true. But if you ever *do* want to get back into other film making...maybe Teresa can help you."

"Yeah, I'd be happy to!" said Teresa.

Luke sat back. "You know – I might take you up on that."

"But Morgan, how could you *ever* live without him?" asked Chief.

She shrugged. "Honestly, if he needs to go up to Vancouver for a few weeks out of the year, that's fine. I can find an alternate."

Luke turned to her. "Am I so easily replaced?"

She kissed him on the cheek. "Of course not. I just don't want you to get bored."

That seemed to satisfy him, and he and Teresa started a conversation of their own about cameras and lighting.

The dinner passed much too quickly, and once she got home, Teresa knew that she couldn't delay her final task any longer: it was time to call her parents.

She'd prepared a script of sorts – talking points and things she didn't want to forget to say. With it in hand, the phone call went...about as well as expected, which is to say, not well at all.

It started with her mom answering the phone and cheerfully asking, "How far are you? What state are you in now?"

Teresa cleared her throat. "Not far, Mom. I mean – I'm still in Washington state."

"What? Did your car break down? Let me get – "

"No, Mom. My car is fine. But what I called to tell you is – the thing is, I'm not coming home."

There was silence.

Then the yelling started.

Teresa hated every moment of it – she hated that she was making her parents upset, and she hated disobeying them. She hated feeling like there was a rift between them, and knowing that they felt bad, too.

She remained calm throughout, though, and stuck to her script.

She was glad that she'd prepared something. There were a few key phrases she repeated throughout. "I love you," "I understand that this isn't what you wanted," and of course, "I am not going to change my mind."

Her mom reiterated the threats of cutting her off financially, then enlisted her dad to stress the seriousness of the cascade of mistakes that she was making.

Teresa held strong, and after almost two hours on the phone, she decided to end the call.

"I know that this isn't what you wanted, and I do respect your opinion. But I've made a decision, and I'm going to stick to it. I love you."

After hanging up, she felt drained. Connor asked if she wanted to go for a late evening walk, but she declined, and instead decided to camp out on her air mattress and write some of her feelings in her journal.

She'd also written a plan for the next six months. After talking to Elena, she'd gotten in touch with Elena's editing friend who said he'd be happy to take her on and give her a chance. He seemed *much* more sane than Chet, which was already a win.

Once Teresa finished writing out her thoughts, she fell asleep and slept for almost ten hours – the best sleep she'd had in weeks.

The next morning, Amanda had to leave early for a meeting in Seattle, but Morgan and Jade treated Teresa to a decadent breakfast of homemade pancakes, scrambled eggs, waffles, and a mushroom and cheese strata.

It was all too much, but she could see that Jade in particular was very similar to her mom – she showered people with love and food so they had no question as to their place in the world.

Teresa wished that there was something that she could do to thank them for their overwhelming hospitality, but she didn't have much. For the rest of the week, she did make dinner for everyone, which they seemed to appreciate. She wasn't a great cook, but she could follow a recipe.

Meanwhile, she and Connor set up plans for their move to Vancouver and their new accommodations. As promised, Connor was able to find her a place to stay that she could afford on her modest salary. Most of her roommates were girls who worked in the tourist industry there; Teresa was excited that she wouldn't be around film people all the time. It'd be a nice change of pace to mix it up.

She was surprised at how effortlessly Connor was able to arrange all of these things. He was a great planner, and she knew that those skills would help him with his new business. He became animated whenever he talked about it – whether it was about securing a business loan, or buying supplies, or planning out routes.

It seemed like they were going to be off to a good start. Connor's friend Tyler had already formed relationships with many of the other boat and touring companies in the area. They shared information about the currents, whale sightings, and other tips that were important for any new business. It seemed like the outdoorsy people were being just as welcoming to Connor as the film people were being to Teresa.

There were still moments when Teresa would wake up and couldn't believe what she was doing – and that she was planning out her life almost entirely on her own terms. And it was working!

Sure, maybe she would fail. But she wasn't desperate anymore. She'd experienced failure once and survived it. She now knew that she could survive it again.

The Friday before they planned to leave, Connor and Teresa took a walk along the shore of Lime Kiln Park. They held hands and stopped frequently on whatever welcoming-looking rock they found, taking time to admire the beauty in front of them or to watch a passing seal or eagle.

Teresa had never felt this way before – she'd never felt so secure. It seemed like everything had fallen into place all at once – though it took a lot of discomfort, anger, and even one break-in to get there.

That reminded her. "You never told me what happened with Lenny breaking into your mom's house?"

Connor let out a sigh. "Yeah. About that. I think he's getting some charges brought against him – nothing huge. From what it sounds like, he can't wait to leave the island."

"And rejoin the mob?" she said with a laugh.

"To be honest, I think so, yes."

Teresa stared at him with horror. "Really? That's so... creepy. I thought it was all a joke."

"I don't know much more about it – and honestly, I don't want to know."

Teresa shrugged. "That's good enough for me. I'm happy to close that chapter of my life for now – and on zombies for a while."

Connor laughed. "Me too."

They stayed at the park until sunset, watching the beautiful show in the sky as the yellows, pinks and oranges took over their view until everything faded to a dark, soulful blue.

Perhaps she didn't know exactly what she was doing, but for once in her life, she knew that she was on the right path. And somehow, she managed to find the right person to take this adventure with – someone who had been on many adventures before.

She leaned in and rested her head on Connor's shoulder. The best, it seemed, was yet to come.

Chapter 27

"Thanks for everything, Mom. And you too, Chief."

Margie squeezed Connor in a tight hug. "Drive safely! And send me a message as soon as you get there."

"I will," Connor said, trying to break the hug.

Margie let out a sigh before releasing him and turning to Teresa. "I packed a cooler of snacks for you too, Teresa. Hank already put it in your car."

She smiled. "Thank you Mrs. Clifton – thank you for *everything!*"

"All right, both of you get out of here before Margie makes any more meals for you."

Connor laughed. "Okay. And don't worry Mom – Vancouver's not that far. This might actually be the closest I've been in years."

Somehow that didn't make her feel any better. She'd gotten used to having Connor around for the past few months and she would miss him terribly. But at least he wouldn't be floundering and looking for his next step in life; and perhaps Teresa could remind him to charge his phone.

"Yes honey, good point," she said. "You're so close that I can come and visit you soon. Be good!"

Margie took a step back and stood next to Hank. He put his arm around her shoulders and squeezed her tight as they watched Connor and Teresa get into their respective cars and drive away.

Margie felt like she had a golf ball stuck in her throat.

"It's always hard when another bird leaves the nest," Hank said. "Even if they leave, then come back, then leave...then come back. Always hungry."

She let out a sigh. "Somehow it never gets any easier."

He kissed her on the top of her head and took her by the hand. "Come on. I got something for you."

"Oh, do I get my own voyage on the Marine Patrol?"

He shook his head. "Not today."

Hank led her into the house and disappeared for a moment before returning with an enormous wrapped present – it was flat and topped with a large, red bow. It was so big that Margie couldn't even hold it – Hank had to set it on the table for her.

"What's the occasion?" she asked, smiling up at him.

He shrugged. "Another glorious day that I get to spend with you?"

She studied it for a moment. Margie liked to guess what presents were before she opened them. This looked like some sort of painting – but of what?

She carefully reached for a corner, delicately removing the wrapping paper. "Did you wrap this yourself?"

"Of course not, it's much too hard to wrap something this big. Plus I don't think we have any tape."

She stopped to look at him. "You know you can *buy* tape at the store!"

"That's not the issue," he said, waving a hand. "The issue is I don't know where it lives. Or where the bows are. And this needed a big bow."

She laughed and kept peeling away the wrapping paper – first a small strip, then two large tears until it was almost completely unwrapped.

Margie gasped when she finally realized what it was – a picture of all of the kids in front of the barn.

"Hank! You're going to make me cry!"

"That's not what you're supposed to do! I wanted to make you feel *better.*"

She stared at the canvas in front of her. All of the kids were in motion – except for Tiffany, of course, who struck the lone serious pose. Jade was jumping up in the air, Connor was pretending to surf, and Amanda and Morgan looked like they were in the middle of building a two-person pyramid. "When did you even take this picture?"

"When Tiffany came for her birthday."

Margie nodded – she did remember Tiffany wearing that outfit. "I love how wild they look."

Hank smiled. "I have a serious one, too, but they insisted on taking a crazy one. And I thought you'd like it better."

"I love it." She paused. Hank's son Jacob somehow made it in, too, despite the fact that he was all the way in Australia. "Hang on – is that Jacob there?"

"Yeah," Hank chuckled. "Morgan photoshopped him in."

"How did I not know that this was happening?"

"It wasn't hard. I had Luke distract you with questions about how you made Tiffany's cake."

Margie laughed. "I *did* think it was odd that he was so interested, but I didn't suspect a thing!"

"I guess Luke can come in handy sometimes."

She kissed him again. "I love it sweetheart, thank you."

Margie was about to suggest that they find a spot to hang it up when the front door opened.

"Honey, I'm home!" called out a familiar voice.

Margie and Hank looked at each other, puzzled, before their visitor walked into their line of sight. It was Mike!

"You can't just keep doing that!" Margie yelled as she rushed over to give him a hug.

"Well I told you that you should change the locks," he said with a laugh.

Hank and Mike shook hands.

"Why are you grinning like that, Hank?" asked Margie. "Did you know that he was coming back again?"

Hank shook his head. "No – this time I had no idea."

She put her hands on her hips. "I was wondering when you'd come back and update us."

Mike put his hands out. "Here I am, your wish is my command."

"Well if you have a few minutes, maybe we can have some coffee or tea? Are you hungry?"

"Coffee would be nice."

She herded them into the living room before going to the kitchen to make coffee for Mike and a pot of tea for Hank and herself. She also threw together a few sandwiches while the water boiled – she had no idea how long Mike planned to stay, but there was no need for him to go hungry.

Margie joined them in the living room and set everything on the coffee table. "So what can you tell us?"

Mike took a sip of coffee. "Not much. Yet."

"I knew that you FBI guys were slow," Hank said, frowning, "but I didn't know you were *that* slow."

Mike laughed. "I had to go back to New York and make myself known – you know, to throw Lenny off of my trail. It seems that he kept quiet about seeing me here, which is good, but I'm not sure he's convinced that he didn't see me."

Margie nodded. "And Hank installed a new security system, so we should be safer."

"Or you can just keep that daughter of yours around, Hank," Mike said with a wink. "Anyway, we've been looking into the connections here. Things aren't really adding up."

"What about that guy Connor was talking about? That Mr. Benzini?" asked Margie.

"That's where things get interesting. He's not involved with the mob. At least, we didn't think he was – until now."

"Who is he?" asked Hank.

"From what we've found so far, he's a boring bureaucrat. He mostly does political advising – he's worked on a few campaigns here in Washington state and a few in DC. From what's available publicly, he looks squeaky clean."

Margie leaned in. "But what did you find when you looked deeper?"

"I haven't been able to look deeper," Mike said with a sigh. "He's not committed any crimes. Not that we know of, at least."

"So what, we have to wait around and hope that nothing else bad happens?"

"For now," Mike nodded as he took a bite of a cucumber sandwich. "Oh this is delicious, what is this?"

Margie smiled. "I get those cucumbers from the farmers market. And the spread is something I made, but stop changing the subject."

He laughed. "I'm sorry, I'm not changing the subject. I don't want you to worry. We'll keep a close eye on the island for anything suspicious. I'm still working on removing myself from the New York scene entirely."

"Are they suggesting retirement for you?" asked Hank.

"I've been suggesting it for myself for some time," Mike replied. "But now, I'm not so sure if I want to leave just yet. There have been some missing links for years – I wonder if this could be the beginning of the answer."

"The answer to what?" Margie leaned in, sure that Mike would need to whisper the next part.

"Well, I can't tell you," Mike said, at a totally normal and non-whispering volume. "Not yet, at least."

She crossed her arms. "You have no idea how frustrating that is."

"Believe me, I do," he laughed. "I can only tell you the bare minimum to keep you safe. Plus whatever you found out on your own, which hasn't been insignificant."

Margie sighed. "All right. Are we going to change the locks then, Hank?"

He shook his head. "Then how will Mike be able to drop in and surprise us like this?"

"Don't worry." Mike held up a hand. "Changing the locks won't really stop me."

Mike said that he preferred to stay until it was dark, so Margie and Hank had the delight of spending most of the day with him.

Mike had never been one to share much about his own life, but he was happy to listen to the happenings on San Juan Island since he'd been absent.

After he left, Hank and Margie settled onto the couch in front of the TV with the goal of finding a movie to watch.

"What are the chances that the mob will come back to San Juan Island?"

Hank shrugged. "Do you want my real answer, or the one that'll make you feel better?"

"That tells me all I need to know," she said with a sigh. "And speaking of birds leaving the nest – what are Amanda's plans? I graduated from physical therapy, so she doesn't have to be stuck driving me around anymore."

"That," he said, "is something I'll have to count on you, my dear, to find out."

"You didn't seem to have a problem talking to Connor! And he never likes to talk about serious things."

"I caught him in a weak moment. I'm surprised that he listened to me, actually."

"All of the kids take you *very* seriously," Margie said.

"Yeah right," Hank chuckled. "Did you know that they've been taking turns sending boxes of donuts to my office for the last two weeks?"

"And they didn't even tell me about it!" Margie laughed. "Whose idea was it to go after Teresa in that boat?"

"You know – we came up with that together."

"Well, I can try to talk to Amanda. I think she's enjoying living with the girls and being back home."

"I think so too."

"Now the question is, do I need to lure Rupert here from London..."

Hank turned to her. "Please don't. I can't stand that guy."

"Really? You never mentioned it before."

He turned back to the TV. "I knew he wouldn't last."

"Well then, I think it's time for me to put my matchmaking hat back on."

Hank groaned. "How about you put your movie picking hat on first?"

Margie laughed and kissed him on the cheek. "Fine. I'll see what I can do."

Epilogue

The first thing that Amanda saw when she opened her eyes was Morgan's face.

"Rise and shine buttercup!" Morgan whispered, grinning widely.

Amanda groaned and pulled the blanket over her eyes. "Why so early Morgan?"

"Because," she said, pulling the blanket back down. "It's sort of my fault that Saltwater Cove is part of the Westcott Bay Music Festival this year, and it *happened* to fall on Margie and Hank's anniversary."

Amanda rubbed her eyes. "I'm sure they don't care. Plus the festival doesn't start until noon."

"I know, but I decided that we should all bake a cake to make it up to them."

"Let me know when it's time to decorate and I'll throw some icing on it for you."

"You're so silly!" Morgan bounced the bed, forcing Amanda to open her eyes again. "You probably want to get ready anyway because we have some surprise visitors coming this morning."

Amanda sat up. "Oh?"

"Yep! Connor and Teresa just texted that they'll be here soon – Connor wanted to surprise his mom."

Now that was something worth getting up for. Amanda got out of bed, showered, and was in the kitchen helping

Morgan when she realized that Morgan might've made the whole thing up. She was about to accuse Morgan of being a liar when Connor and Teresa arrived.

Amanda hugged them both and immediately accosted Connor. "Why didn't you tell me that you were coming?"

"Because we both decided late last night that we were going to do it, and then got up super early this morning to make it on time."

Amanda frowned. That was a pretty good explanation, and quite believable from Connor. He and Teresa had their hands full in Vancouver.

Amanda felt like she was closer with Connor ever since they'd helped their parents recover from their injuries. He'd kept in touch, as much as Connor could, keeping her up to date on his business and new life. Which is why she was particularly irked that he hadn't told her he was coming!

"I guess I believe you," she finally said.

"Don't blame him," Teresa interjected. "I thought I'd have to be up all night working because of a deadline, but it got pushed back!"

"Nothing like putting off work for later," Connor said with a wink.

Teresa laughed. "It's fine. Things are, knock on wood, actually under control."

Jade walked in, still in her pajamas. Apparently Morgan's urging hadn't worked on her. "Oh! You're here! I was – "

"Yes yes, it's very nice to see you all," Morgan said. "But I've got a complicated cake that isn't going to make itself."

Amanda laughed. "All right, I'll get back to helping you."

Though Amanda was more distracted in her cake making while catching up with Connor and Teresa, it made the time go quickly. She was excited to hear all about Connor's company, and he was more willing to share than usual.

"So are you still glad that you went to Vancouver then?"

Connor nodded. "Absolutely."

"Good. I'm glad."

"What about you? How's work going?"

Amanda shrugged. "The same. Not bad."

"I don't think you can call your job 'not bad' unless your boss leaves."

"Well *that's* never going to happen," Amanda said with a laugh. "It's okay though – we've got a few big clients coming in over the next quarter, but after that, things should calm down."

Connor studied her for a moment. "If you say so."

It took almost two hours to craft the fondant and chocolate decorations that Morgan envisioned for the anniversary cake, but once they were done, they packed everything up and loaded into Jade's car to head over to the barn at Saltwater Cove.

Amanda volunteered to sit in the back seat, squished between Morgan and Teresa.

She was happy that Connor and Teresa had found a new start in Vancouver. Amanda toyed with the idea of moving there too, or *anywhere*, in case there was some sort of opportunity for her, but she decided against it. For some reason, she wasn't ready to leave San Juan Island.

Was she convinced that another mob guy was going to break in and attack Margie?

Well, sort of. Morgan also supported the idea that things would keep happening on San Juan Island; Amanda had to pretend that she didn't agree with her, even though she knew more about the mob situation than Morgan, and Morgan was pretty spot on with her suspicions.

Amanda felt guilty that she couldn't tell her more – nothing about Uncle Mike, or about the connections there. Her dad stressed how important it was to keep things quiet, though it seemed like Morgan was never more than a few steps behind.

"Morgan, why didn't you make this cake the way I wanted it?" asked Connor.

"What do you mean?"

"You know, big enough for me to jump out of."

Morgan let out a huff. "And ruin my chocolate work? No way. You can jump out of the trunk and yell 'surprise' for all I care!"

"No one will be getting in the trunk," Jade said sternly.

"What if Amanda gets in and jumps out, throwing ninja stars?" asked Morgan. "Is that allowed?"

"No, definitely not," Jade said, parking the car.

Amanda laughed. She didn't care that her reputation had gone from yielding a taser, to nunchucks, to now ninja stars – she was just glad to be part of the group.

Everyone else got out of the car and she sat in silence, savoring the moment.

Introduction to *Saltwater Memories*

Nothing ruins a happily ever after faster than curiosity...

Amanda's move to San Juan Island did not turn out like she'd hoped. Losing her boyfriend was bad enough, but watching her career fall apart is almost more than she can handle. So, she's willing to admit it might be time to pack up and move on. But then a charismatic property manager with ties to a mystery she's dying to unravel shows up and everything changes.

Will's only goal is to manage his client's new properties. Falling in love is nowhere on his to-do list. But there's something about the grumpy, quick-witted Amanda that makes him forget what he's supposed to be doing on the island. Little does he know she has an agenda of her own—one that could cost him a lot more than his job if he's not careful.

On an island full of secrets, does true love stand a chance? Amanda and Will are about to find out...

Saltwater Memories, book six in the Westcott Bay series, is a sweet, wholesome, sometimes funny, sometimes suspenseful, and always inspirational romantic women's fiction read. It features a heroine who can't abide a mystery, and a hero who is more mysterious than even he realizes. Get your copy today and get ready to fall in love with your favorite series again!

Would you like to join my reader group?

Sign up for my reader newsletter and get a free copy of my novella Christmas at Saltwater Cove. You can sign up by visiting: https://bit.ly/XmasSWC

About the Author

Amelia Addler writes always sweet, always swoon-worthy romance stories and believes that everyone deserves their own happily ever after.

Her soulmate is a man who once spent five weeks driving her to work at 4AM after her car broke down (and he didn't complain, not even once). She is lucky enough to be married to that man and they live in Pittsburgh with their little yellow mutt. Visit her website at AmeliaAddler.com or drop her an email at amelia@AmeliaAddler.com.

Also by Amelia...

The Westcott Bay Series

Saltwater Cove

Saltwater Studios

Saltwater Secrets

Saltwater Crossing

Saltwater Falls

Saltwater Memories

Saltwater Promises

Christmas at Saltwater Cove

The Orcas Island Series

Sunset Cove

The Billionaire Date Series

Nurse's Date with a Billionaire

Doctor's Date with a Billionaire

Veterinarian's Date with a Billionaire

Made in United States
North Haven, CT
09 September 2023

41344015R00139